MW01592671

THE LIGHTNING WITCH TRILOGY

THE LiGHTNiNG PROPHECY

BOOK ONE

BY

EMILY CYR

Crushing Hearts and Black Butterfly Publishing

Novi, Michigan

Cover Designed by Najla Qamber Designs

www.najlaqamberdesigns.com

Editing by Red Road Editing / Kristina Circelli (www.circelli.info)

Proofreading by On the Mark Editing / Susan Turner (www. facebook.com/onthemarkediting)

Editing for CHBB / Elizabeth A. Lance

Formatting by J.R. Roper

Though some of the places are real this is a work of fiction. The names, characters, and situations in this work are the product of the author's imagination. Any resemblance to any persons living or dead, or situations are merely a coincidence.

—For my husband Ashley.
Thanks for saying, "Why not?"

—And special thanks to, Allie, Yvette, Casse
and Shauna. Because damn…

THE LIGHTNING WITCH TRILOGY

THE LiGHTNiNG PROPHECY

BOOK ONE

BY

EMILY CYR

"No one is so brave that he is not disturbed by something unexpected."

—JULIUS CASEAR

PROLOGUE

ALTHEA HAGAN

13 December 1992

My daughter, Delaney, was born during a thunderstorm. I should have known that the next four years of her life would be much like the storm on the day of her birth. My daughter, like a thunderstorm, is beautiful. She has my husband's brownish-red hair and his wide smile that seems to light up the world. She has my gray eyes and my small turned-up nose. And, much like a thunderstorm, she scares the hell out of me.

"Mrs. Hagen. It looks like your cat will be fine. I want to keep him here for a few days though," Dr. Greenburg said in a brisk tone. We had been seeing this vet for several years, and several cats. "It looks as though the cat got a nasty shock."

"Oh yes, Frankie must have bitten into an electrical

cord," I lied. *Please buy this lie.*

"Possibly, but the cat had scorch marks on its back," she retorted, clearly not buying a damn thing I was saying.

"I don't really know what happened. My daughter started screaming when she was playing with Frankie. I was in another room and then I rushed him here." That was part of the truth anyway. She seemed to buy this partial truth, thank goodness.

The lie was I knew just what happened to Frankie. Delaney got upset when he scratched her and then she touched him. When she gets upset or overly excited, she sends out electrical charges. I had never seen anything like it before. This was the first time she'd hurt someone or something, though. She was getting stronger and I honestly had no idea what I was doing. I felt like a failure as a mother, not just because I had no idea how to handle my child, but also because I secretly wished she were normal.

I left the vet and headed home in a hurry. I had to get back to Delaney. Mrs. Adams, our elderly neighbor, was watching her and there is no telling if Delaney could unknowingly hurt her. *God, what parent worried about their child electrocuting the babysitter?* I knew Robert may not want to admit it, but our daughter was a witch. We needed help dealing with her. We needed help controlling her. We needed help not getting hurt around her.

"Mommy!" Delaney's eye's sparkled when she saw me. She ran up to me and hugged my knees. *Ouch. At least it was only a slight shock.* "Where's Frankie, Mommy?" She looked up at me with puffy red eyes and a tear streaked face. Her hair was a halo of brown cotton going out in just about every direction.

"Hey, baby girl. Frankie is staying at the doctor's office. He saw a few friends there and he wanted to spend the night," I said, smoothing my hand over her wild hair.

"Oh, okay." She gave one of her Earth-shattering smiles and ran into her toy room. I turned to Mrs. Adams and gave her a weak smile.

The seventy-something-year-old woman stood up and walked over to me, placing her wrinkled hand on my face. She smelled of wintergreen and mothballs.

"Oh, honey, you look so sad. Is the cat okay?" Her voice was so small and sweet, it pulled at my heart and made me want to cry simply at the sound of it.

"Yes, he's fine. It's just been a long day."

"Okay, dear, but you call me if you need me. You hear?"

I nodded and said, "Yes, ma'am. Thank you so much for watching Delaney."

She shook her head and smiled. "No worries, dear, she's a good child. A bit clumsy, but good."

I walked Mrs. Adams to the door. After she was gone I sat at the kitchen table with the telephone in front of me. I was vacillating. Do I make the call or do I try to handle my child on my own? Why, as a parent, was it so hard to say we are in over our heads? After debating with myself for twenty minutes, I picked up the phone and dialed the number.

"Aye, what do ya want? It's dinnertime." Mil's Irish lilt rang loudly over the speaker. I glanced at the clock over the stove to see it read 4:04 P.M. Seemed a bit early for dinner, but fine.

"Hi. Mil, it's Althea." There was silence for a heartbeat.

"Ah, yes, Georgina's girl."

"Yes. I am glad you remembered me. How are you?"

"Pfft, girl, out with it. I know you did not call to chat with me." Her tone was brisk and to the point. My chest began to tighten and I could feel my heartbeat in my hand as I gripped the phone.

"Mil, I-I-" I took a deep breath, mentally chanting, *you can do this.* "I think my daughter, Delaney, is a witch."

I heard her take in a deep breath. "Aye, well, you know you need to take her to the Coven for training. They will…"

"Aunt Mil," I cut her off, "she has power I have never seen before."

"Girl, there are only four powers she would have."

"Aunt Mil, she electrocuted the cat." There, it was out there. Now someone else knew. There was a long pause.

"Tell me everything."

And I did. I told her how we thought it was static electricity. But, that we quickly learned it was tied to her emotions. I had known she was a witch for some time; however, my husband kept saying to give her time and she would grow out of it. After I was done, I voiced my biggest admission.

"Mil, I'm scared of her."

"Give me your address, girl. I'll be over in a few hours."

I did as she requested then asked, "Should I call the local Coven?"

"No, for God's sake don't do that." The sound in her voice had a bit of worry in it. I looked over to see Delaney playing with her dollhouse. In that moment, I could only see the perfect child I held four years ago. I hung up the phone after saying good-bye and waited for Mil to get here. I waited for help.

Three hours and fifteen minutes later, Mil was standing in my kitchen. I sat the teapot on the burner and got out three bags of Earl Gray tea. I went to get two mugs, but there were none to be found. Clearly they were all in the dishwasher. *Great.* I began putting the dishes away.

"Aye, girl, let me help you," Mil interrupted, coming to grab a pot off the top rack. There we were, both not talking about the reason she was here, trying to put off the inevitable.

The inevitable came bounding into the room.

"Mommy, I can have a cookie?" Delaney asked, looking up at me expectantly. Her eyes found Mil and froze on her.

"Hello, little one." Mil walked over to Delaney and bent down to look at her.

Delaney firmly looked at her shoes, trying to avoid the new person in the room.

"Delaney, this is Mommy's Aunt Mil. She's your aunt

too!" I said, trying to get her to open up. Her eyes met Mil's and stayed there. A big smile spread across her face.

"I never had an aunt before. Can I have cookie?" Delaney looked up at me with such hope in her wide eyes. That expression always tugged at my heart.

Just as I was reaching for the cookies, Mil waved a hand at me and in a stop gesture.

"Oh no, little one, no more cookies," Mil said. What was she playing at? All she was going to do was upset Delaney, then she would ... oh. The smile fell from Delaney's small face and was replaced with a frown.

"But, I want cookie!" Big, fat tears spilled over her cheeks.

"I'm sorry, Laney girl, but they are all gone. I ate them all." Mil's voice carried a sorrowful tone. Delaney's silent tears became heartfelt sobs. I thought for a moment nothing would happen and Mil would think I was insane. But, just then, sparks began to fall from Delaney's fingertips. Mil's eyes went wide at the sight of the falling electricity. She looked at me not in horror, but in sympathy.

"Oh look! Mil left one more just for you!" I said with tears in my eyes. Delaney's bright smile returned to her face as she caught sight of the cookie.

"Oh, Aunt Mil, thank you! Thank you, Mommy!" she said as she grabbed the cookie and returned to the toy room.

"Come, let's sit at the table," Mil said, grabbing my hand and pulling me to the metal chair. She didn't look horrified.

Why? Hell, I felt horrified.

"Can you help us? Please?" I knew I sounded frantic; it's how I'd felt for the past two years when this first started. "I love Delaney. I-I-I just don't know how to raise her."

"Hush now. I know you love her. I also know you are not equipped to deal with her power." Her tone was so matter of fact.

"Even for a witch, this power isn't normal, is it?" My voice was a bit shaky. Hell, finally I had someone who would help us! Maybe we could be normal.

"No, it's not. But, I need you to listen to everything I am about to tell you. There is a prophecy that has been handed down from within the inner circle of the Coven. It is said that the words came from the mouth of the last known human sacrifice of the Druids. It is told that the prophecy came from Taranis, the God of Thunder himself. Back then, the Druids who were the first witches needed to perform these sacrifices to make sure their powers were maintained through all of time. After time passed, the act was outlawed. With the Druids not being able to perform the sacrifice, their powers changed into what we are today. Druids had a great amount of power. They not only could control the earthly elements, but they could shift forms into beasts. But, once the sacrifices stopped, the powers diminished and split."

"Okay, so what does any of this have to do with Delaney?" This was all going over my head. What could any of this have to do with my little girl?

"It was said that the lifeless body of the sacrifice spoke after her death. It was written that a child would be born of the God of Thunder and Lightning. But, child, I cannot tell you all of the prophecy just yet as I need to get to know the child and I need to fully understand it myself. But, what I can tell you is she is supposed to bring the end of all witches."

My mouth hung open. Was she ill? Crazy, perhaps? I sat there with my mouth agape, just staring at her. I mean, what else could I do? After a story like that? She told me next to nothing, except that my child would bring an end to the witches. It sounded batty. I didn't say that, but I wanted to.

"Stop lookin' at me like I'm the crazy one!" she said, clearly offended at my shocked expression. I shut my mouth with an audible click.

"Mil, you just told me my daughter is going to wipe out every last witch. Oh and you can't tell me the rest? I'm not sure how to take that," I replied, honestly taken aback.

"Don't believe me? Fine, take her to the Coven and explain it to them. They will not only take her from you, but they will likely use her powers for their own purposes or kill her. And they will give you less explanation than I have." Her tone was so pointed I felt the sting of the words against my skin.

Mil's eyes told me she was one hundred percent sure of every word she spoke. It made a shiver run down my spine.

I got up and walked over to the entrance to the playroom. Delaney sat at a small table with a purple plastic tea set on it. She was currently pouring imaginary tea in her green bunny's teacup. I looked over at Mil, who stood in the doorway watching my little girl.

"So, what do we do?" I asked as my throat began to close with a silent sob.

"I will leave my position in the inner circle, and I will train her to the best of my ability. We agree to never tell her any of what I told you, and..." she looked at me, her gaze hard and very, very serious, "we run."

DELANEY HAGEN
ONE

"HEY, RONALD," I SAID IN A SHAKY VOICE.
"Oh, hey, Delaney. What's up? Is the store okay?"
Ronald asked nervously.

Deep breath, Delaney, deep breath. Just tell him what happened and maybe, just maybe, he won't fire your ass.

"Um, yeah, Ronald, everything is fine. But …," I couldn't spit the words out. Maybe I could just tell him the store was robbed. And instead of guns they used flamethrowers and blew up the register. Setting the money on fire? Seems logical. *God, I'm in such deep shit.*

There was a long pause and I could hear the buzzing of the phone connection.

"Delaney, hello? Are you there?" Ron shakily questioned.

"Oh yeah, sorry." I felt the bead of sweat roll down my back and pool at the base of my spine. *Get this shit together,*

I chanted in my head. "Um, well, the cash register kind of … blew up."

There was a pause the span of a few heartbeats.

"Ronald? Are, are you there?" my voice squeaked out. I sounded like a three-year-old. *Way to instill confidence in your employer. Sheesh.*

"I'm sorry, did you just say the register BLEW UP?" he raged into the phone.

My mouth gaped in shock at his fury-filled reaction.

"You have got to be kidding me!" he continued.

My heart began to race. I could feel my power rise along with my fear and anxiety. Electricity began to jolt from my fingertips. I clenched my fists, trying to control the lightning. My nose filled with the scent of burnt plastic and fried electronics. *Calm thoughts, Delaney.* I opened my eyes to focus on a fixed point on the wall. Several heartbeats went by as I tried to bring my heart rate down. I slowly felt the lightning ease from my body, and belatedly realized I had dropped the phone and could hear Ronald's muffled frantic screaming pouring out of the speaker.

I picked up the phone and held it about six inches from my ear, where Ronald could clearly be heard. Ronald was prone to hysterics when it came to his vinyl or when I was involved. I couldn't really blame him, as this wasn't the first time I had blown something up.

"Hi, yes, I'm here and no, I'm not kidding. Ronald, calm down. I don't know how this happened. It just did," I lied.

"What about the vinyl? Is the vinyl okay?" He sounded utterly and completely panicked.

"Yes, Ron, the records are fine," I said calmly. I tried to hide the panic in my voice even from myself. The last thing I needed was to out myself as a witch.

"Delaney, just close the store and get out," Ronald said in a hurried tone.

"But it's the middle of the day, what-" I was cut off by Ronald's frantic words.

"Leave the keys under the mat and GO," he ordered.

"Ronald, please I need this job. I'm not doing this, it's, it's, it's just happening!" I begged to him.

"Delaney, this is the second time in four weeks something has blown up with you there. Look, go home for now and when the register is fixed, I'll call you. But, if anything else happens, you're gone. I mean it, Delaney," Ronald said in a father-like tone. He quickly added, "The vinyl is okay, right?"

I rolled my eyes at the phone and exasperatedly said, "Yes, Ronald, your preciouses are fine."

"Hey, Gollum was cool. Bye, Delaney," he said before the call ended.

I placed the phone on the receiver and slid my sweat-soaked back down the wall, plopping my ass on the floor. I rested my head on my hand with my palms pressing into my eyes. I had to learn how to control this thing or I was going to burn down a building. I was twenty-six years old. I should have control over my ability by now.

I stood up on wobbly legs and moved toward the door. As I reached it, I slowly turned around to view my current disaster. The register lay in a melted heap of smoking, charred electronics. I could see faint handprints melted into the drawer that dangled down from the base, and could still hear faint popping noises coming from the charred lump. Were those sparks flying from the heap? *Crap.*

I ran past the racks of records and busted through the back office, grabbing the red fire extinguisher and aiming it at the heap. White foam exploded from the nozzle, covering the mass of burnt mess. How did I get here? I mean, I know physically how I got here, but how and when did my life get to be such a damned mess?

The toe of my sneaker caught the lip of the outdated Persian rug and I went flying forward. In an effort to catch myself, my hand tightened on the handle of the fire extinguisher, causing the foam to spray with more force than I thought possible. Yup, this was my life. Lying on a cheap rug, probably bought from Wal-Mart twenty years ago, covered in foam, surrounded by the mess I made.

Slowly, I got up to survey the damage one last time. Now, the glass counter that once held "priceless" - according to Ronald - records was covered in foam. The counter behind that where the cash register sat looked like a snow-covered mountain in miniature. *Yup, when Ronald sees this, I am so fucking fired.* I was better off spraying my own ass with the damned extinguisher. I spared a glance down at myself and the ground. Too late for that. It was time to get the hell out of Dodge.

I opened the front door of the store and was immediately blasted by the heat and suffocating humidity of a Savannah summer. I locked the door and picked up my phone, dialing a number. After six rings I heard a sweet southern voice sound from the speaker, "Hey, y'all this is Sierra. I can't come to the phone right now so…" I hung up the phone. Looked like I'd be huffing it home. If only I could find some other witch in a Coven to teach me, I wouldn't have this issue. Witches, unfortunately, are difficult to find, even if you are a witch.

Witches can be hard to find for a reason, though. It's known we exist, but we are persecuted and made to register ourselves. Humans are ruled by fear, what can I say? Most registered witches live on reservations. But, some witches, like me, choose to live as a human and fend for ourselves. Okay, so reservations might not be so bad, but they stuff us on a plot of land as though we have smallpox and finding a job is nigh impossible because there is a demarcation on your license that states your witch status, including your power and power level. Plus, it's not like there are signs in windows that say, "Witches wanted." Yeah, we were wanted like a rat infestation.

Witches have secret covens over the whole United States. There is also a governing Coven that mediates and -

let's just say it out loud — controls with the iron fist of a god all of the smaller covens and witches. As a registered witch, you are subject to the rule of the Coven and, like any group of bureaucrats, they are corrupt and will use you within an inch of your morality.

Now, there are a few benefits to being with a coven. They help witches come into and control their powers. Most witches can control an element of the earth, such as air, fire, earth, and water, in a minor way, but some can do some pretty amazing things and have a great control over their power. This is the exact reason why I do not have control over my power. I control the lightning. No one knows how to teach me. And if the Coven were to find out about me, well, my new job title would most certainly become lab rat or utensil. I am better than I used to be, but, on occasion, I still tend to kind of blow things up, just a little. In other words, I am a walking disaster.

One cannot just become a witch. You must be born one. Geneticists and scientists have worked for years to isolate the "Witch Gene" and breed it out of existence. But, it hasn't worked. All they have done is found out it's a mutation in the genome and can happen to anyone and happen to any family.

As I walked down the sun-drenched street, my thoughts slipped to my great aunt. Maybe she was right. Maybe I should have continued to move every year. But come on. Who could do that every single year? I was going crazy!

And really, what were we running from? Sure, my great Aunt Mil was all the family I had left after my parents died when I was five. Mil raised me. But, just six years ago, I told her I wouldn't move again. I found somewhere I blended in, somewhere I could appear human. Every year she would just show up and try to make me pack my bags.

"Aye, me girl, it be time we take our leave and I not be leavin' without you," she would say in her stiff Irish lilt, all the while stuffing my shit in boxes.

As I calmly removed my things from the well-used boxes, I would say, "Mil, listen, I am safe here. We do not need to move all the time." This is about the time she would cut me off and say she was my elder and that I needed to show her respect, blah blah blah. Then I would retort with, "Mil, I am too old for you to tell me what to do!" Then there would be tears and hurt feelings. Yes, the Coven would use me, but she had spent years teaching me how to avoid them. I was a grown-ass woman and I needed to start acting like it. And these were all points I told her.

Every time I expounded on these points she scoffed at me, saying, "You, girl, are a silly twit."

I shook my head to try to loosen the thoughts and clear my head of the depressing memories. I picked up my phone to look at the still-blank screen. Where the hell was Sierra? She should have called me back.

I awkwardly shoved the too-warm phone in my pocket. *This Savannah heat and humidity may kill me.* When people come to Savannah they think, "Oh, it's going to be hot." Well, it's a whole other kind of heat. Today, it was about 90 degrees and the humidity level out of 100% is currently 416%. I am not sure how Savannah defies the laws of physics and Mother Nature by having 416% humidity, but it does.

All in all, it took me about an hour to walk home. By the time I got there, my hair and shirt were soaked with sweat and I smelled like I was fished out of a river. And my hair, now it was in a special state caught between an Angora rabbit and lion. This day kept getting better and better.

I peered up to the forty thousand cement stairs that led to my apartment. They were single handedly put on this Earth to kill me. By the time I made it to my front door, I had about two gallons of sweat soaked into my clothes. *Boy, I'm sure I smell like a rose.*

I opened the front door and a whoosh of cold air greeted me. Thank goodness for central air. My apartment was pretty small. It was a one-bedroom studio apartment located near downtown Savannah. I don't do the decorating thing much, so things are pretty sparse. It's mostly Goodwill finds and hand-me-downs. I don't have a flat screen or stereo system. Technology and I have a love-hate relationship. I want to love it, it hates me, and I hate the bills that come from the damages acquired when we have a spat.

The clock read 4:32 P.M. and I still hadn't heard from Sierra. I called her for a third time. This time I left a message. "Sierra, where the hell are you? You were supposed to pick me up from work. By the way, this is D."

Sierra, much like myself, was an unregistered witch. That's where the similarities ended. I was about 5'5 with a slim waist and curves in the right places. I had shoulder-length, mousy brown hair with glints of red. Sierra was 5'10 and beanpole thin with very few curves and beautiful, long, bouncing blonde ringlets. Her eyes were a stunning bright blue while mine were storm cloud gray. She had a nose that on anyone else would look like a beak, but on her long face looked just right, whereas mine was more of button nose that turned up slightly at the tip. I had a round face where hers was narrow.

I settled in for the evening and turned in around 11 P.M. No sense in dragging this disaster of a day out.

I WAS RUNNING. DARTING UNDER THE BRUSH, DODGING trees. My heart was about to pound out of my chest. Something was chasing me. I couldn't seem to focus enough to look behind me and run at the same time.

My skin and fur started to generate their own electrical charges and sparks started to fly. The scent of wild things and dirt flooded my nose, but there was a third scent I couldn't quite place. My thoughts were so foggy and drenched with the need to run I couldn't focus on anything. All I could hear was the rush of wind, my erratic pounding heartbeat, and the snaps of electrical charges my fur was producing.

Wait, my fur?

I took a frantic heartbeat to look down at my running feet and saw large, white, fur-covered paws. Paws? When the fuck did I get paws!

Fear. The third scent that filled my nose was fear. It was my fear and someone else's fear and it excited me.

I woke up with a start and sat straight up in bed. My room was pitch black, but for the small red number radiating from my bedside clock. It read 4:35. The hell was that dream all about? I had been having weird dreams since I was little, but this was the first time I wasn't human in one.

I laid back, trying to get my heart rate down. I lifted up my hands just to be sure they were, in fact, hands. Thank God, two hands. I rested them on my chest, fingering the small hole in my shirt. Hole? Shit, did I smell burnt feathers?

I put my hands in my shirt and inspected the damage. Great, another shirt Swiss cheesed. I blindly stumbled to the light switch. After my eyes adjusted, I saw the real damage. See, this is why I can't have nice things. Or sleep with anyone.

"Ugh," I groaned at the sight of my outline burnt into the bed. Crisped feathers littered the bed and surrounding floor. I pulled open the window to vent my tiny apartment of the smoky burnt smell. This just wasn't normal. Nothing about me was normal. I wanted normal! Even if I were still a witch, couldn't I be an Earth witch? Or Air? No, I was the freak among freaks. I got lightning.

Three sharp knocks sounded at my door. I about peed my pants at the start of the intruding noise. Who the hell was at my door at this hour? I mean, really? I stumbled up, throwing my shirt off and tossing a dirty one on. Hey, at least there were no holes in this one. Right?

I looked through the peephole to see two armed police officers. Oh shit! How did they find me? I began to feel the lightning dance inside me. I held up my hands to see arcs of lightning dance from one finger to the next. Okay, hot sauce, calm down.

Two more short raps sounded at the door. Take a deep breath. I opened the door to see one rather stocky pale man who looked to be in his late forties. Was that mustard at the corner of his mouth? The other man was a serious-looking tall man who seemed to be in his thirties. He had beautiful skin the color of rich chocolate cocoa.

"Sorry for the bother, ma'am, I know it's late, but are you," the tall man paused, looking at a piece of paper. Finding what he was looking for he continued, "Delaney Hagen?"

My heart was about to pound out of my chest. I shakily replied, "Uh, um, y-yes."

"Do you know a Miss Sierra Pierce?"

My mouth fell open. This wasn't about me at all. Worry for myself was quickly replaced with worry for my friend. Eyes wide in shock, I said, "Yes, she's my best friend; is everything okay?"

The two officers exchanged a look that clearly said no, she was not all right. The short man started with a gruff tone, "Ma'am, I am sorry to be the one to tell you, but Miss Pierce was in an accident and…"

I wasn't sure if he stopped talking or if it was the shock of it. But, the next thing I knew, I was sitting on the floor with the taller officer hovering over me. He asked in a relatively calm voice, "Ma'am, are you okay?"

I looked up at him with tears streaming down my face. I didn't say, "No, you moron. Does it look like I'm okay?" but I thought it.

I shakily said, "I'm okay, you just caught me off-guard."

"Ma'am, Miss Pierce has no family in the city that we can tell. You are the only person we can find with connection to her. We need you to come with us to identify her remains."

Remains? What the hell did that mean? When the hell did accident turn into remains? "Remains? What do you mean remains?" I questioned while trying desperately to wipe my nose on my dirt-smeared hand.

"Um, ma'am, we aren't really at liberty to say other than we need someone to identify the remai- er, I mean Miss. Pierce," the short man quickly stated. I knew whatever it was had to be bad because he wouldn't look me in the eye. My opinion of the stocky man dropped drastically. Coward.

I started to get up and a big hand grasped my elbow in

assistance. I gave the tall man a weak smile. That was the extent of the emotion I could grasp at that moment. I began walking to their car when the other one cleared his throat, making me turn to him.

"Um, ma'am, you may want to get dressed before we head to the station," he suggested with a tentative smile.

I looked down to see a dirty shirt that hung down to my mid-thigh and no pants. Shit, had I been talking to these men this whole time without pants on? What the hell was wrong with me! God, oh god, please let me have had underpants on. I did a fast assessment of the situation and, yes, I indeed did have panties on. Oh god, Sierra, and I'm worried about underpants.

"Oh, yes, please give me ten minutes to get ready," I finally said.

Numb. I was just numb. Each hallway I was pulled though seemed to pass by me in slow motion. Hell, I couldn't even recall the drive there. In my head I was there for three hours walking through the sterile hallways.

"Wait here," an official-looking woman said. I looked up at the tall officer and glanced at his nametag; it read P. Marshall.

"Would you like me to stay?" Officer Marshall asked, the sound of his voice breaking the serene silence and making me start.

"Oh, yes please," I replied in a shaky voice. I wrapped my arms around my middle and faced the large window and waited. The heartbeats raced by. What do we have to wait for? I mean, my God. It wasn't her. That's all there was to it. It could not be her.

The woman who asked me to stay here went through a door off to the right of the large window. She walked up to the window in a manner that showed she had clearly done this before. She pressed a button on the wall. Her voice sounded slightly robotic over the speaker. "Miss Hagen, are you ready?"

I looked around, trying to find the damn speaker, but couldn't locate it. I swallowed the lump in my throat and closed my eyes. I thought about Sierra, her bright smile and bouncing blonde curls. Tears pricked my eyes and my throat got tight.

I remembered our first meeting five years ago. We met in the fruit aisle of the local grocery store. The memory made me smile.

"Hey, there!" Sierra said.

"Oh, hi," I replied with a shy smile.

"Look, you don't want that lettuce. See how it's browning around the edges? It's so going to be nasty in like two days," Sierra said with a knowing smile. She took the lettuce from me.

In the process, she grabbed my hand and a small jolt of electricity leapt from my hand to hers. I just knew I was going to have to move now. Damn it, I was always so careful. Here I was with someone I didn't know and I couldn't control my damn power! She could be anyone and I had just outed myself.

"Ouch!" she yelped.

"Oh my goodness, I am so sorry! Dang static electricity!" I said a bit too hurriedly, even for my ears.

She raised an eyebrow at me and put her hands on her narrow hips and began tapping her right foot. I think she knew. I looked around to see if anyone was listening. When I saw it was all clear, I said in a whisper, "Look, I know you know I'm a witch and no I'm not registered and I have the freakiest power you have ever seen. Can we maybe keep this between you and me? Please?"

She gave me a big smile and put her arm around me and said in a bright tone, "Oh thank god! I am unregistered as well. And your power is cool as shit. I think I'm going to like you! I'm Sierra. What's your name?"

I felt a tight grip on my shoulder and it jolted me back to the present. I opened my eyes to find everything blurry with tears. I took a deep breath and reminded myself. This isn't her. It can't be. I looked at the woman though the glass. She seemed to have a tight, annoyed expression on her face. I gave her a stiff nod.

The woman walked over to the table and pulled the sheet down. She did this with brisk practicality, a motion all too familiar for her. My eyes reluctantly slid from the woman to what lay beneath the sheet. I had to step closer to the window to make out that it was indeed a person.

The person on the table was missing her right arm at the shoulder; it was ripped out of its socket. It looked as though someone had been gnawing on her. Her face was a mess of what looked to my untrained eye to be bite wounds and deep gashes. Her throat was simply gone. And her beautiful bouncing blonde curls lay lifeless and matted with blood. Knowing without a shadow of a doubt it was her, I turned quickly away from the gruesome sight. Bile rose. Oh god, I was going to lose it right here on this guy's shoes.

My eyes darted quickly about the sparsely furnished room. My mouth began to water, knowing what was coming. Chairs, tissue, table, ah! Trash can! I darted for the trash can, tripping on the rug and nearly falling into the damn thing. I dry heaved twice and then I lost it. I threw up until all I had left in me was the air in my lungs and the lightning behind my eyes.

DELANEY HAGEN
TWO

B Y THE TIME I GOT BACK TO MY APARTMENT IT WAS
bright out. My head was reeling with thoughts of Sierra, so sleeping was out of the question. *What now?* Sierra
didn't have family for a funeral. I sat on the edge of my bed
with my head in my hands and heels of my palms pressed
into my eyes. *What would Sierra want?* Sierra was a Water
witch, and a powerful one at that. An image of her trying to
help me control my power popped into my head.

*"Look, see right here?" Sierra said, pointing to the golf-ball-
sized orb of water in her palm. "Your focus needs to be on the
element, not what you want the element to be," she calmly said*

"What does that even mean?" I question.

Sierra rolled her eyes while saying, "Call up your lightning."

*I closed my eyes and focused on my core. I centered my
thoughts and focused on pulling the lighting that danced inside*

me. I opened my eyes and my palms, not having to look at my hands to know the lightning arced and popped between my fingers.

Smiling, Sierra said, "Okay, first of all that's just about the coolest thing I have ever seen. Second, putting your element in the form of a ball is one of the first things we learn. You need to think of it like an extension of yourself. Feel yourself in the lightning. Feel yourself move and form into the shape." She motioned for me to try it.

I thought just like she said. I focused my intent and will into myself, pulling myself into a ball and focusing on forming the lightning into a bright sphere. I opened my eyes and saw a sparking ball of lightning. There was a faint scent of ozone becoming ever more present as the sparks and arcs popped and crackled. I looked up to Sierra's bright, smiling face saying, "She can be taught!"

Tears were streaming down my face at the memory. I couldn't just sit here and do nothing for her. She did everything for me. She taught me when no one else could or would. She was so much more than a friend; she was a sister. She was part of my whole, and now here I was trying to find a way to fill the void she left behind.

I am not religious; well, not really anyway. But, there was one prayer that I knew and maybe by saying it, it would be enough to soothe the ache I had in my heart. I stood up, trying to gather my resolve. *I would* do this. I would do this for Sierra. I grabbed my keys and walked out the door.

My car was a dark-green 2000 Toyota Corolla. The damn thing was falling apart around me. It had so many dents and dings, I lost count years ago. Thank goodness the internal parts all still worked.

It only took me about twenty-five minutes to make it to Tybee Island then walk to Little Tybee. I picked Little Tybee because it's a place only locals really know about and Sierra and I went every chance we could get.

The sun was setting and it cast an orange hue on everything, making it look otherworldly. The sun gave the waves a slight burnt-orange tone and the sand looked almost brown. I looked down at my sand-covered feet and thought they, too, looked orange in the strange light. The lightning inside me stirred at the setting sun. *Oh, that's right, yesterday was a full moon.* A witch is at their most powerful on the day when the moon is at its fullest. *No wonder I blew the damned register up.*

I reached into my pack, getting out a large clam shell. It was my mother's and was used at her and my father's Requiem. I went to the shore and placed the shell at the surf, letting the waves lap over it. Once the shell was filled I made my way back over to my towel and other things. I gingerly set the shell full of water down as not to spill it and pulled out a picture of Sierra. It was my favorite picture of her, from when we went camping two summers ago, both of our smiling faces completely drenched. I laughed, Sierra the selfie queen. That trip had been one of the best moments of my life.

I was always complaining how it was easy it was for normal witches to be surrounded by their elements. But, for me, it was impossible.

One rainy Sunday, Sierra drove me about an hour outside of Savannah. After questioning Sierra within an inch of her life, we pulled up to a field of pretty much nothing. It was covered in mostly dead grass. Upon further inspection of the area, it was really quite pretty. The field with dead grass was surrounded on two sides by huge green oak trees. Protruding from the ground, placed about twenty yards from us, were two huge metal rods.

"Okay it's pouring out and you bring me here. Uh, why?" I questioned. I was honestly baffled.

With a knowing smile she turned to me and said in her thick southern accent, "Because, goof bucket, we are camping here."

I looked at her and raised my eyebrow in question. It was pouring rain, and while I could survive a lightning strike I had serious doubts that she could.

"We will set up here and those rods, my dear, are lightning rods. And this is a lightning storm. Well, in two hours it will be. You know lightning can be hard to predict."

I just sat there, dumbfounded. And my eyes were most definitely filling up.

That night, I was struck by lightning. And it was the most amazing feeling I have ever had. With every strike, my core filled with untapped, raw power. Every inch of me tingled. I walked up to the tent after about two hours and just stood there, looking at Sierra thought the open flap. I'm sure I had a big, goofy grin plastered on my face.

"Girl, I'd hug you, but I'd be afraid to electrocute you."

"Ha! Yeah, it's a power surge. Focus on your core and pull the power from your fingertips, toes, and top of your head and compress all of the power to your core."

I closed my eyes and focused on pulling the power inward. Lightning sometimes had a mind of its own. Imagine training a tiger to do a back flip into a pool whilst singing Yankee-Doodle-Dandy. That's about how easy it is to control lightning. While it's under control most of the time, it had the ultimate power and was capable of reverting back to its nature.

"Is this what it feels like when you're near water?"

"Like you're so full of power you could explode? But, the mere fact that you can control something so wild just grants you such happiness and peace?"

"Yes, exactly!"

She smiled. "Yes, and now, padawan, you can harness the force too." And with that, we both cracked up laughing.

I sat the photo next to the shell and next pulled out a pair of leopard-print high-heeled shoes and a T-shirt that belonged to Sierra. I closed my eyes and thought of Sierra and concentrated on slowing my breathing. Out loud, I said, "Sierra was a witch of the water, thus to water I bring her."

I took the shell and dropped three drops of water on each item. "Go easy, Sierra. From water we are born, and from water we die. Go now, and find peace in the great land. Your loved ones surely await you. Go easy, and know I loved you."

And so it was done; with the release of the water she was free. I think she would be happy it was me who performed her Requiem.

The drive back to my apartment was long, mainly because I couldn't get my power to settle down. *What now?* I couldn't help but feel mad. Hell, mad? Mad was too meaningless a word. I was furious. Something had tried to eat her and whatever it was, I was going to find and turn to ash.

By the time I made it to the parking lot of my apartment, my hands were shaking and lightning was sparking and crackling in my hair. I had to calm down. I took the keys out of the ignition and set them on my lap with a jingle. I closed my eyes and thought of Mil, then opened my eyes with a start. That's it! I'll go talk to Mil. God, she knew everything. That's where I would start, then to the police station. I would not let this go. I calmly opened the door and got out of my car, feeling better knowing I had a plan set in my head. I could do this. I would do this.

My mind was on that plan, so I didn't see the giant wall that blocked my path and I barreled right into it. Trying to not fall on my ass, I sent my hands out, searching for something to grab onto. I found nothing, but a strong arm grabbed me around the waist, steadying me. Arm? Wait, I didn't remember there being a wall here before.

Before I could think clearly I backed away from the stranger and called the lightning to my hands. I looked up to see this person more clearly. In front of me stood a man. A rather large, muscular man. His short, blonde hair was mussed and his caramel-colored eyes were trained on me with the focus of a laser.

With a short, audible "pop," I forced the lightning back into my body. A shiver ran down my spine. All the while, this hulking brute of a man stood staring daggers at me. Another shiver went through me that had nothing to do with my power. Wow, this man had a strong, square jaw with light-brown stubble shadowing his cheeks. He looked as if someone had fashioned him from stone with a chisel. His full lips were set in a flat white line and his brow was furrowed in contemplation and assessment. *Is he seriously measuring me?* With a flick of his eyes he completed his assessment and looked as if he found me wanting. *Well, if this ass thinks he knows me, he's got another think coming.*

I raised my eyebrow and squared my shoulders with my own assessment. Other than the waves of cocky and asshole this guy had wafting off of him, he was sexy as hell. He had muscles for days. Wait, make that months. He had broad shoulders that beautifully cascaded into a chest most men and women would kill for. Then there was his stomach, and I would be willing to bet all the king's horses hid a 266 pack. The black, silk button-down shirt and charcoal-gray slacks hugged him in all the right places and then some. My eyes may have lingered on the apex between his legs a fraction longer than they should have. But, God himself wouldn't blame me, because this dude was built like a brick house and it had been a long time. A really long time. Like forever.

I realized a little late his eyes were fixed on me. He had an amused expression plastered on his face. In fact, he looked down right smug. Well, I guess he has a reason to be smug. There he stood, looking like a GQ ad, and I had on blue jeans with a pale-yellow ribbed tank top. I looked like an ad for a K-Mart blue light special. I narrowed my eyes to his and gave him my "I'm so not impressed" look, and opened my mouth.

Instead of saying something polite like, "Oh my gosh, I am so sorry. I didn't see you there," my mouth bypassed my mental filter and, well, words started falling out.

"Look, Macho Man Randy Savage, I'm sure it's polite to stand in someone's way in the cave you oozed out of, but it's not polite in this world. So, how about you let me pass." No, I did not just say that. God, I didn't even know this guy but he rubbed me the wrong way. A small voice in my head felt the need to chime in, *"I bet he could rub you the right way."* *Go shove it, horny voice!* I felt my cheeks turn a warm shade of pink. *Great. I'm such a moron.*

Macho Man's eyebrow raised and the corners of his mouth twitched upward. I narrowed my eyes at him and spat, "Do you speak English or caveman?"

"I speak English just fine," he said with a slight southern accent. Just the sound of his warm liquid voice seemed to caress my skin and settle inside me. I swallowed down the rush of heat his voice brought and gathered my too-fast waning resolve and attacked again.

"Well, could you move? All of you," I gestured to him, "seems to be blocking me from getting to my apartment." God, why did this guy seem to bring out the hostility in me?

"Macho Man Randy Savage? Really? I like to think I'm more of a blond Rock if indeed I had to pick one," he said with an annoyingly chipper tone.

I paused to think about it. No, Chris Hemsworth. Now that I really considered it, he did remind me of Thor. Lord help me, the man was beautiful. I shook my head, trying to extricate my libido from the current situation.

"Look I've had a shit day and I would love to go to bed. You're literally standing in front of my door. See my problem?" God I even sounded bitchy to myself, so that must be bad.

"Look I'm not sure who you are but…"

"Reid," he said, cutting me off.

"What?" I replied, blinking up at him. Good lord how tall was this guy? I didn't think of myself as short, but next to Macho Man here, I was a damn child's dolly.

He cleared his throat. "You said you didn't know who I was, so I'm telling you. My name is Reid. Reid Jamison. And you must be Delaney Hagen."

I thought I might have stopped breathing. How the flying fuck did this guy know my name? Sweat dripped down my back, leaving an icy chill in its wake. I took a quick step back. He gave me a smile that could only be seen as predatory.

"The Coven sent me to investigate the death of Sierra..." he trailed off, obviously trying to think of her last name.

In a low, but very controlled voice, I said, "Pierce. Her last name is Pierce. Was, I guess it's was now." Tears threatened to blur my vision, but I would be damned if this man would see me cry. "And since when did the Coven give three shits about an unregistered witch?" I said in my iciest tone. I mean, really. The Coven couldn't care less about unregistered witches. In fact, they would have us jailed if they could. He had to be lying.

"Could we maybe step in and talk in private?" he asked, putting emphasis on the word *private*.

Is he kidding, or does he think I am a moron? I honestly had to re-evaluate my thoughts on this hulk of a man. He wasn't a witch. I knew that for sure. He didn't have the telltale feel of a witch. Every witch had a power base that came from within them. To other witches, it felt like a dull thrum of power. It's like feeling a second pulse in your core. From what Mil had told me, it's the magic calling out to one of its own. This Reid guy didn't have that, but he wasn't human. I wasn't sure what he was, but I surely wanted to figure it out.

"What are you? You're not a witch. I know that for sure.

35

And I know the Coven would never hire a human. And you don't feel like a human. So, what are you?" I widened my stance and put my hands on my hips and looked up at him with my best impatient look. He raised an eyebrow at me and the corners of his perfectly formed mouth started to twitch in an upward motion. He seemed as if he was trying not to laugh at me.

Oh, you have got to be kidding me! *What a condescending asshole*. That was it. I was going to electrocute the shit out of him, both metaphorically and literally. I narrowed my eyes at him and said, "Look, buddy, until you provide me with some proof the Coven sent you, I'm not letting you in my anything."

His eyes widened at my statement.

That's when it hit me. *Oh my God, he thought … Oh sweet mother of God*. I could feel my face turn red and even a few sparks fell from my fingertips. I saw his eyes flick to my fingers and I quickly put them behind my back. I then met his eyes and my breath caught at the caramel-colored orbs that seemed to spark with green. He was the one who broke the silence.

"Ms. Hagen, I will show you my private investigator's badge and I can answer your questions when we go into your apartment. For now, that's all I am looking to get into."

With that last comment, I surely thought I'd die or at least faint. Had he said "For now?" as in that might change later? I looked down at the badge and it seemed official, but what did I know? For all I knew it could have been an arcade prize. But then he pulled out a white business card with his name, "Reid Jamison, private investigator" on it and pressed into the card was the official seal of the Coven, a round Celtic knot surrounding an ornate tree of life.

I hated that damn symbol. It represented the four elements witches could control. I was an outcast even on the damn seal. Mil was well known with the Coven and they knew she had a great niece, but, to their knowledge, I had no power. If the Coven ever found out what I could do, they would use me. Of that I was sure.

I looked up at him and into those eyes, then stepped toward him. He didn't so much as blink. In a slightly husky voice I said, "Well you're still in my way and my apartment is on the other side of you." I place my hand on his chest and it was way too warm for a normal human. I thought he might burn me. Why did I touch him? I swallowed and continued, "So I'm going to need you to move the hell out of my way." I let my hand drop from his chest, but not before I felt his heart rate speed up slightly. He slowly moved to the left of me, flattening himself against the wall. His eyes were flecked with green again, but I couldn't think about how beautiful they were. I had to get this over with and start my own investigation.

We sat at my kitchen table. It was small and bought second hand. Most of my things were.

"Do you want coffee?" I asked. God, I just wanted him

out of my house. Why did I ask him if he wanted coffee? I must be going insane.

"Sure, black is fine," he said in a clipped tone.

I pulled out my French press, already-ground coffee, and stovetop kettle. As I put the water on the gas stove I heard a grumble from behind me.

"Don't you have a coffee maker?" Reid asked from behind me.

Ugh. How to answer that question? Well, Reid, I picked this apartment for its gas stove and water heater and I don't use electronic appliances because I'm a walking, talking electronic disaster area. Finally, I settled on saying, "No, the coffee is better this way," which was very true.

A few minutes later and coffee in hand, I sat at the table. I said, "So, Mr.-"

He cut me off with, "Reid. Call me Reid."

"Okay, Reid, what are you? Because I know what you're not. You're not a witch and you're not human."

"No I'm not. And haven't been for a while now."

I just stared at him, blinking. I mean, what did you say to that? Okay, I'm not human, not technically, so who am I to judge?

"I can feel your power, but it's not like a witch's power. It's not more or less; it's just different - more feral? Maybe. So, what are you?"

He leaned across my small kitchen table and got within five inches of my face. He smelled like a pine forest, summer heat, and man. My heart began to race with his nearness. He parted his lips and gave me a very predatory smile. Don't they say don't run from a predator? My head told me to run like hell. Apparently, there was a breakdown in communication because my feet didn't move. *Am I prey?*

"I, my dear, am a shape shifter, as we like to be called, but think of me as a werewolf. And the Coven hired myself and my partner to handle this matter as discreetly as possible."

He didn't back away. He just sat there, staring at me. He seemed to be waiting on something, a reaction of some kind. A shape shifter or werewolf. I was officially living in *Twilight*. Oh my God, this guy looked serious. I laughed in his face. I mean, what else could I do?

"Are you done yet?" he said, looking mighty annoyed.

"Yes, I think so. But really, what are you?" I asked, half snickering.

He leaned even closer and his eyes went green. Those beautiful caramel-colored eyes freakin' turned green, as in traffic light green. I abruptly stood, knocking the chair over behind me and scrambling over it. My foot caught on the leg of the chair and I went down, but I would not be a victim to this, this *thing*.

On hands and knees I scrambled over to the pantry door, but before I could stand up I saw him move. He calmly walked over to me, moving the chair out of the way, and offered me a hand. Yeah, right. Was he nuts? I called the lightning to my hand and raised it to him in threat. I was going to barbeque his ass. Brick house or not, his ass was grass. I didn't stop to even think about the Coven or what they would do if they found out about me.

Between shaking lips I said, "Get the fuck away from me or this ball of lightning is going to turn you into beef jerky!"

He raised an eyebrow at me and flicked his glance at my hand and took two small steps back. He put his hands on his hips and peered down at me.

"Now, Ms. Delaney, the question is, what are you?"

DELANEY HAGEN
THREE

S HIT. WHAT WAS I THINKING? I SLOWLY PULLED THE lightning back into my core and just sat there looking up at Reid.

"Look, I know it's a shock, but I'm here for some information to help catch this murderer, not to hurt you. So, I'm going to walk over to you and help you up. I would also ask you to refrain from beef jerkying me."

I tensed as he slowly walked over to me and reached his hand out again. I grabbed his hand and, as I did, I realized I forgot about the residual electricity on my skin.

He quickly jerked his hand back and wailed, "Whoa, ouch, holy hell, woman!"

"Oh damn, sorry, I forgot. Residual charge. Are you okay?" *I'm such a moron.* But, damn, he took that whole shock. A normal person would have been laid out on the floor pissing himself.

He looked back at me as he rubbed his hand and fore-arm. God, those eyes. And his mouth. *Get it together, Delaney!*

"Uh, yeah, I'm good. But what the hell kind of witch are you? I mean, I know you guys can control water, fire, earth, and air, but lightning, that's new." He looked about as dismayed as I felt. *Well, you know what, big guy? Good.* I just found out there really are things that go bump in the night.

I sighed. "Look, can we keep this between you and me? If so, then yes, I control lightning," *or it controls me most days*, "And no. There are no others like me and no, I absolutely do not want the Coven to know about me."

I looked up to see him studying me. His gaze seemed to pierce my soul. I shifted in my seat. "Well, so how did you become a werewolf? I mean, are you born or made or is it like *Twilight*? You don't look Native American," I said, trying not to smile.

He rolled his eyes at me and smiled a real smile. It completely lit up his face. He had the kind of grin that made you want to return the gesture. I had to stop myself from grinning like a goof ball.

"I'm not Native American. Really, you're comparing me to a tween? Insulting!" he said jokingly.

"No, I was not born this way. Werewolves are made. And before you ask, no, you cannot be turned, only humans can be. And it's not as simple as a bite. We can only be turned on or near a full moon. Although, this isn't one hundred percent, let's call it ninety-eight percent correct. The person has to die."

"Wait, they have to die? What, do they rise in the morning? You don't drink blood, do you?" I quipped. I could not seem to stop myself from being a complete ass with this guy.

"Really? I'm not sure I should respond to that, but no. Stop interrupting me and I'll tell you."

According to Reid, not only did the person who is being changed have to die and not wake up until the next new moon, but only fifteen percent of people wake; most tend to stay dead. No one really knows how werewolves came about, but there are theories. Reid's theory was that, much like witches, it was a rare genetic mutation. But, like the theory with the witches, it didn't feel right. My power felt like it knew his power. Hard to explain, but I felt like there was a bigger truth to be had.

Hollywood apparently did get a few things correct, such as the length added to their lives and that they were weakened by silver, but the only way to kill them was, as Reid said, "We can be killed if our heads depart from our shoulders. There's really not much coming back from that."

My head was reeling and I must have had a complete look of incredulity on my face because Reid furrowed his brows at me and sat back in his chair.

Finally, I seemed to find a few words. "So, you turn into a wolf, okay. Prove it. I mean, your eyes do some freaky change to green thing, but I mean, changing into a wolf? It's kind of farfetched. Oh and how old are you?"

"You sure do ask a lot of questions. You sure you're not the P.I.? Okay, I'm eighty-three; I was turned when I was twenty-eight." In a low, controlled voice he said, "No, I will not tell you how I was changed, nor will I change for you. It's painful on both accounts." There was a warning in that tone.

He looked pained as he said it. "Oh, okay, um, look, I'm sorry…" I mean, what else could I say?

"Look, I'm sorry I've been such an ass and that I almost fried you. It's just been an awful few days and you just told me the things in my nightmares were real. I need to adjust." I got up from the kitchen chair and walked over to the battered, green-plaid couch and sat down. God, was I really ready to talk about Sierra? Ready or not, here I come. That's how the song goes, right?

"What do you want to know about Sierra?"

Reid got up from his chair and paced over slowly, then sat down next to me. When he moved like that he looked like he was stalking his prey. Sexy as hell. Or scary as hell, depending on my sanity level, and currently I wasn't feeling very sane. My heart sped up with just his nearness. *Traitor of a body*. His hand brushed mine and there was a small static spark.

"Oh man, that's going to take some getting used to," he said with a quick smile.

"It doesn't happen all the time. Like here. See, nothing,"

I said, putting my hand on his and giving him a shy smile. His skin was so damn hot. "Why are you so hot?" As soon as the words fell out of my mouth I wanted to shove them right back in.

With a knowing smile, Reid said, "Ha. Well I do try."

"You know what I mean!" Ugh, open mouth, insert foot. *Ugh*.

"It's part of what I am. My temperature runs about three degrees higher than a human's. Delaney, I need to ask you about Sierra."

The smile on my face utterly died.

"Okay, what do you want to know?"

"I need to know about her last few weeks. Was she seeing anyone? Did you meet any new friends? Was she acting scared?"

"God, no. She was always happy. She was like sunshine to my storm clouds. I talked to her maybe four days ago? And she was super happy. She said she met this new guy and she was trying to get him to ask her out. I left her a message just the other day because she was supposed to pick me up from work, but I got off early and..." I trailed off. I just couldn't do this. I would not cry. Deep breath, take a deep breath.

"Do you know this guy?"

"No, but Sierra wasn't stupid. She was a pharmacy tech, for God's sake. She worked in that CVS right off Derenne and Abercorn. This guy came in asking about something

45

and they got to talking. She just told me he was smoking hot. And that she gave him her number. That was the last I heard. I don't know if she ever went out with him or not."

"Is there anything you can tell me about the guy?"

I just stared at him. I still had this nagging question. Swallowing hard, I dared to ask the question again. "Look, I want to find the ass munch who did this, but why did the Coven hire you? As far as I knew the Coven couldn't care less about unregistered witches. And the Coven doesn't like to go to outsiders for anything, much less help. So, why?"

As he began to answer, I noticed my hand still lay atop his.

"Because, Delaney, the Coven wanted the best to find out who or what has been murdering witches along the east coast. And remember I am not human, so they came to me, as I tend to have a very good nose."

I'm sorry, did he just say witches as in *plural*?

"What do you mean by witches?"

He flipped his hand so he could hold mine in his. My hand looked like a child's hand next to his. Why wasn't I pulling my hand from his? I hardly knew this guy. Yet, here I was letting him closer than I had let most anyone.

"The Coven has been hiding it, but there have been no less than ten witches found dead along the east coast. Their bodies were all ravaged just like Sierra's. None of the witches were currently registered. But they were at some point."

"Black hair and beautiful eyes, that's what she said," I

blurted, because I didn't even know what to think. "So you're telling me there's a serial killer who's targeting witches?"

"Wait, what do you mean black hair and beautiful eyes?" he said, letting go of my hand to emphasize the point.

"That was all Sierra said about the guy she met."

"That's it? You're sure?"

"Yes." My life is a bad mystery novel, I swear to God. Reid's mouth firmed into a straight white line. I narrowed my eyes at him and asked, "What is it you're not telling me?"

He paused to look at me. He seemed to be deciding on whether or not he could confide in me. Well, he better get his shit together, because no was not an option.

Finally, he spoke. And he did so with deliberation, "The other reason the Coven hired us is that they are convinced the one hunting and killing these witches is a werewolf."

And there it was. The thought I hadn't wanted to admit the whole time he was here. The image of Sierra's ravaged body was seared in my head. Every time I closed my eyes, it was her body lying out on that table I saw. Her body looked as if some kind of animal had been gnawing on it.

God, what have I gotten myself into? Every cell in my body was screaming to my brain. They wanted to send the directive to my feet to run for safety. Hell, run to Mil, tell her how right she was and to go back to living that bullshit of a half-life. *What about Sierra? What about the life that was stolen? Shit, make that lives.*

"Well, what do we do next?"

47

Reid looked at me as if I had four heads that were questioning him about what tampon I should be using.

"Look, Reid, if you think for one damn second you're going to be leaving me behind in this investigation, you're in for a rude awakening. I am doing this with or without you," I said, crossing my arms over my chest. If he thought for one second I'd be cowed by him, he clearly didn't know me.

He furrowed his brow and stared at me.

I wasn't giving up on this. "I guess I'll go looking for the big bad wolf myself. Now, where did I put my little red hood?"

"Oh for fuck's sake, woman!" He threw his hands in the air in resignation. "You won't give up, will you?"

"Nope, she was my best friend. And I flat-out refuse to let that friendship die just because she's gone. That's not what friendship is. I will fight because I'm the only one left to do it." Damn, where was my soapbox?

"Look, there was a lot going on with this case, so I asked a friend to help me out. He's an alpha from Atlanta. He is in DC right now looking over a few things there with another murder in this case. So, until he gets here, you can tag along. I don't want you out there trying to get yourself killed … or worse."

"What's worse than death?" I said with a confused look. I mean, death is pretty damned final. There's really no coming back from it.

There was a pained expression on his face. "Not dying

48

can be substantially worse than dying."

God, I wished I hadn't even said anything now. Just as fast as the pain came to his face it seemed to leave.

He gave me a slight smile and said, "Look, I'm meeting with the investigator tomorrow and I can meet you afterward and go over what I have found out. Because Sierra has been found to be a witch the police have turned over the investigation to the Coven and that's me."

"Well, it's better than nothing." I wrote my number on what seemed to be the only thing I had lying around, an old Walmart receipt. "What time are you meeting with the investigator? That way I know when to meet you after?" I gave him my most honest smile.

"Ten A.M. So, I'll meet you at noon. How about I buy you lunch?"

"Great, sounds like a date." The words just fell out ... He raised one of those beautiful tawny eyebrows at me. Belatedly, I tried to correct myself. "Oh, I mean not a date as in a date, but, oh never mind." This man seemed to scramble my brain and erase my brain-to-mouth filter.

"I'll see you tomorrow, Delaney," he said as I closed the door behind him.

There was no way I was letting him meet that investigator without me. I wasn't sure what I looked forward to more, the look of shock on his face when he saw me there tomorrow or just seeing his face. I really needed to find a way to tame my inner slut, because this bitch was going to

get me into some serious trouble. Reid Jamison was off limits. No matter what that slut thought.

REID JAMISON
FOUR

WELL THAT WAS...UNEXPECTED. DELANEY HAGEN was supposed to be just another interview. She was anything but just another anything. I could not get my mind off that female. Her light-brown hair kept catching the light just right and her *body*. And those storm-cloud eyes. She was sexy as hell. When she grabbed my hand and shocked me, my cock had a plan of its own and I had a hard time not jumping on her. Humans and witches were off limits. I would not watch them grow old. Witches may live longer than humans, but weres have them both beat. But, damn she had fire. I had not lived this long to just be undone by some female. I had to get my mind back on the case I was being paid to solve. And being paid quite a bit to solve. Hell, maybe having a witch help would prove useful, and with powers like Delaney's, the possibilities were simply endless. Possibilities like pinning her to the wall and fucking her until we were both senseless. *Uh, yeah I am not going to do that. Focus, Reid.*

Ten murders all along the east coast, over the last five months on and around the full moon. Clearly someone was trying to change witches to weres. This was one little fact I had neglected to tell Delaney. She had enough surprises for one day. I honestly found it a bit surprising that she did not know about werewolves, but she did seem a bit sheltered. It was common knowledge that only humans can be changed into werewolves.

Why in the hell would someone be killing witches in hopes they would rise were? There had to be another reason for the killings. My head was reeling. *I wonder what information Mitch is digging up in the DC area.* Mitch, the alpha from Atlanta whom I worked with here and there, was, all in all, a close friend. While I worked better alone, I had a feeling from the start I would need his help.

I am a lone wolf, by choice. But, the Coven waved a serious amount of cash at me, so I decided Mitch was essential to this investigation. At least half of the first murders had been in Atlanta. I had gotten nowhere with leads in the Atlanta area because Mitch had his pack so tight and tied up. Even with Mitch's help, we had pretty much gotten absolutely nowhere. I had known him for years before this and even with that, I did not trust him 100%. But, then again, I didn't 100% trust myself. I chalked my distrust up to the fact that he was an alpha and I was a lone wolf by choice.

I was still sitting in my Jeep Wrangler in the parking lot of Delaney's apartment complex. I started the engine, but before I shifted into drive I pulled out my cell phone and dialed Mitch's number.

"Saldana," Mitch's voice sounded tinny.

"Hey, Mitch, whatchya got?"

"Hey, Reid, not too much here in DC. There was only one murder here and the chick didn't seem to have too many friends. Seems like a dead end. How's the murder in Savannah going? Any possible leads?"

"Yeah, one. The girl had a close friend and the friend said she gave her a slight description of the guy." The silence spanned for some time. I thought we had gotten disconnected. "Mitch, you there?"

"Oh yeah, I am just surprised. This guy has been picking people who have no one, so this could prove to be a huge break. What was the description?" Mitch answered hastily.

"Black hair and beautiful eyes," I replied.

"Not much to go on, but it's more than we had before. I'm wrapping things up here and will have the files sent your way. I want to meet this witness, see if I can get anything out of her. I need to stop in Atlanta for a few pack things, but I should be there in a few days."

"Sounds like a plan," I said, hanging up the phone.

Well, I would see him in a few days, but if he thought he was going to get his hands on Delaney he was dead wrong. There was no reason I should feel so protective over Delaney, but man, I did. And the thought of Mitch talking to her or hell, even touching her, made me want to rip something apart. I put the car in drive, got on the Truman Parkway and headed for my hotel near the river. Maybe the drive and tonight would help clear my head of Delaney Hagen.

MUCH TO MY CHAGRIN, THE NIGHT AND SUBSEQUENT morning did little to rid my thoughts of that woman. Right now my mind needed to be on the case. I tried to empty my thoughts of everything but the case, so I did the only thing I could, I opened up the engine of my Wrangler and floored it. Finally, the case. I had to figure out how all ten of these girls were linked and this guy killing them had to have missed something. No one was perfect.

It only took me about ten minutes to get the Savannah Police Department. I could have walked it, as Savannah is a walking city and my hotel wasn't far from the SPD's location on Habersham. The heat and humidity in Savannah would be killer for a normal human, but for a were, since our core body temp is a few degrees hotter than normal, it was even worse. So, driving was the only way to go.

I pulled into the parking lot and that was when I saw her. She wore a knee-length white skirt with a red silk shirt that was sleeveless. The shirt had buttons up the front and the collar looked more like a blood red scarf around her neck. Her shoulder-length, mousey-brown hair - was that red when the light hit it? - was delicately billowing in the slight draft. She was leaning on a beat-up POS green Toyota.

My first thought was how much I wanted to see that shirt on the floor and that skirt around her ankles. However, my second thought was that I was going to certainly kill her. *Damn this woman!* My shock had to have been plastered across my face as I parked my car next to hers. I honestly didn't know if I was more shocked to see this female standing there or my reaction to her. The wolf was far too close to the surface for my liking. I did not spend years taming and caging this animal inside to have some little witch undo me. I could not afford to let her undo me. I took a deep breath and got out of the car.

"Del-"

"Wait, before you say anything. You need to understand something. Sierra was all I had. I mean, she was everything. I can't just sit and wait for the things that go bump in the night to come find me. I need, Reid, NEED to do this. I won't talk, I'll do what you say, but I will not be left behind."

Had she really cut me off? This female was indeed undoing me. If she were a wolf I would certainly put her in her place. But, she was right. This girl was all she had. Her eyes were filled with pain, hurt, and regret. If it were me, ugh, I mentally groaned. Sometimes I wanted to throttle my inner sensical voice.

I cleared my throat and spoke, "Delaney, yes you can come, but please, please don't say anything unless I ask it of you. We shouldn't be here long. I am just picking up the files and getting any notes and thoughts they have. They are humans and you know how humans feel about witches."

A genially bright and grateful smile lit up her face. And in that moment I knew I wanted to be the one who could cause such a beautiful reaction. I think I was being undone whether I liked it or not. I had to remind myself that, no matter what happened with Delaney, I could not let the wolf gain the upper hand. I was more than the animal I kept chained up inside of me. It took me years to figure that out and countless losses along the way.

The building was all brick with a green awning. From outside, the building seemed to be less than state of the art, but hey, who was I to judge? As a private investigator I had made a name for myself, but not a fat wallet. I tended to not work well with others, so the money I made was all on me. All of this tended to isolate me, and as a lone wolf, that was how I prefer it.

When I walked in the door, a gust of wind surrounded me and pushed the scents of the area around. There was the scent of heated pavement, trees, Spanish moss, stale office, and then there was Delaney's scent. She smelled of ozone and gardenias. Her scent alone stirred things in me that should be left dormant in this situation. *Reid, the case.*

The lobby was fairly minimalistic, with a few chairs and closed doors. There was a receptionist's window with a female officer glancing my way. I gave her my best *I should be trusted* smile and said, "Hello, my name is Reid Jamison. I have an appointment with Lieutenant Shaun Harris."

The African-American woman looked at something on the computer and said with a broad smile, "I'll let him know you and um, your partner, are here, honey."

We went to sit down in two of the chairs facing all of the doors, putting our backs to the wall with the door we walked in.

Delaney leaned over and whispered in my ear, causing a brief wash of heat to head southbound. "Why didn't you tell her you were from the Coven?"

"Delaney, sometimes I forget just how young you are. You have lived among humans and away from the Coven your whole life. Humans have a prejudice against witches. They would just as soon ship you all somewhere else and not have to deal with you. This is the main reason my people haven't come out as of yet. At least you can live a halfway normal life. We wouldn't have that ability. We would be lucky to live as second-class citizens." She sat staring at me, looking as if what I said had not occurred to her.

"I am well aware of the prejudice from both the humans and the Coven. I have run from all of them my whole life. My parents died when I was little and my great aunt raised me and we had to live outside the Coven for fear they would use me. Had we gone to the Coven, we would have to register and live on a reservation and struggle for every bit of life we would want to live. My whole life has been a half-life."

Before I could form more than a coherent thought, the door nearest the reception window opened and out walked an overweight, forty-something white man with only what could be considered sparse brown hair on top of his shiny head. If the comb-over was in style, this guy would be the Brad Pitt of the look. The balding man wore khaki pants with a white button-down shirt. Clearly, whatever he had for breakfast included grape jelly, as evidenced by the large stain on his bulbous belly. This man had to be no taller than 5'7.

"Why, hello there. I am Lieutenant Harris. I assume you were sent to pick up the files and talk about the Pierce murder case?" he said with a deep southern drawl. I happened to glance at Delaney as she stiffened at the mention of her friend's name.

"Hello and yes."

"Good. Good. You and your partner can come with me." At the word *partner* he paused to run his eyes over Delaney, lingering on certain parts of her body that I would love to bash him over the head for noticing. I had to stifle a growl.

"Okay," was all I could manage as a reply.

We walked down a narrow hallway into a fairly large open room crammed full of tiny cubicles. It reminded me of one of those mazes they put mice in.

"Ah, here is my humble abode," he said, stopping at one of the cubicles. The desk was littered with empty coffee cups that read J. Christopher's, and other like restaurants.

There were empty condiment packages strewn about the files and if Jimmy Hoffa's body was found to be in this man's workspace I would not be surprised a bit.

"Please have a seat," the man said while gesturing to two dilapidated office chairs. I sat and glanced up to Delaney, who was still standing.

"I'll stand if it's all the same to you," Delaney said, clearly put off by the state of Harris's work space.

"Sure, honey, you're welcome to stand there all day long if you like." Harris gave Delaney another once-over. That was it, I was going to have to kill this guy. I was going to have to stuff his body under that desk with old Jimmy. Delaney didn't seem to be bothered by his remarks.

"So, the Coven has hired a private investigator to solve this?" he asked in a disgusted and disapproving tone.

"Yes, they hired me a month ago," I replied evenly.

He began rummaging around on his desk, gathering papers and files. After about five minutes he said, "Okay here is everything, including notes and the coroner's report and contact information. They should still have the body if you want to go look at it. I guess she's your problem now." This guy had to be the most unorganized slob I had ever seen.

"Great, thanks. Any other information you would like to add to aid to the investigation?" I said in my best *I want to get the fuck out of here* tone.

He looked at me, then to Delaney, then back at me. He sucked his teeth then said, "She was just some witch.

They aren't really worth my time. Witches are always getting themselves into some mess here or there. Look, these witches don't belong here. I'm sorry this girl got hurt, but at least now she can't go around unregistered causing all kinds of problems for humans."

Oh shit. This ass was going to die, but I wasn't going to be the one to kill him. I looked up at Delaney and she had a big smile on her face, and for some reason that seemed to be slightly frightening.

"Reid. Sir, that's all I got for you."

Dragging my eyes off Delaney, I said, "Yes, thank you. If I can get your card in case I have any other questions, that would be great."

He reached in his pocket and handed me his card. I picked up all of the stained files and loose notes and that was when I smelled it. Ozone and burnt plastic. Before I could look up I heard Delaney's sweet voice chime, "Oh my goodness. Lieutenant Harris, your laptop. It seems to be smoking and, oh my goodness, it's melting!"

I looked first at the smoking heap of what once was a laptop then to Delaney. I narrowed my eyes at her and sent her a silent message with my expression alone that said, "Really! That was mature." She looked at me, shrugged, and replied just as silently, "What? Did you expect less?"

This whole time we had this little exchange Harris was losing his shit.

"Oh god. No. Someone, hey, a fire extinguisher!"

I got the files and pushed Delaney toward the hallway we entered from. Just before the door closed I heard Harris yell, "Oh God, not my phone too!"

I didn't know if I should be mad, amused, or a little afraid of this firecracker standing next to me. I grabbed her arm and dragged her out the front door just as the sprinklers went off in the whole building.

I raised an eyebrow at her. I mean, really. She stood there with her hands on her hips just glaring at me.

"Was that necessary?" I finally said.

She seemed to think about the question then looked me dead in the eyes and said, "No, but it sure was funny as hell." She gave me her biggest smile. Then she started giggling with little snorts and gasps of air.

Lord, this woman, I couldn't help but smile. "Come on, woman, let's go grab a sandwich and go back to my hotel and we can go over this."

I tried not to laugh. God, she could end up being fun. Maybe her being off limits should be rethought.

DELANEY HAGEN

FIVE

A S MUCH AS I LOVE THE GODFATHER FROM ZUNZI'S, I really wished I'd waited to eat until after we had all of the victims' files spread before us like some morbid buffet. *"Why, hello there! Welcome to the morgue, we have several murders for you to visually feast upon. What would you like, a mutilated blonde? Redhead? Brunette? We have them all,"* I mentally quipped. *God, I have the worst sense of humor on the planet.*

I must have looked green because Reid leaned over and said in a low voice, "Hey, you okay?"

Was I okay? What kind of question was that? I was in shock. I had never seen anything like that. Well, not outside of a movie. The fact that I knew this was real did a number on me. I closed my eyes tight, willing the fear and disgust away. I would not cry. Why did these images hit me so damned hard? I was such a coward. What had I gotten myself in to?

I felt Reid's warm fingers under my chin urging my face upward so I would look at him. I slowly opened my eyes and found his caramel eyes peering into my depths. He looked at me as if he could see every single bit of me. There was no fear in his gaze, no judgment like I see all too often. I blinked and turned my head, breaking his light hold on my chin. It was too much. Him, he was too much.

"I'm fine. Let's just figure this out and get this ass hat." An expression ran over his face. On a normal person I would call it hurt, but he was so damned foreign to me I'm not sure I knew what it was. As fast as it crossed his face it vanished, and I wondered if I had really seen anything or not.

I looked down and saw nine case files before me. "Wait, you told me there were ten victims. Where is the tenth?" I asked, trying to break the tension that was fairly palatable.

"Remember I mentioned my partner? Well, Mitch was tying up some loose ends in D.C. while I'm here. He's the local alpha from Atlanta. Because half of the murders happened in Atlanta, I asked him to help me with the investigation." His tone was clipped on the last bit. I wasn't altogether too sure he was pleased he had to ask for Mitch's help. He seemed like a bit of a loner. Like when he was in school he would get a report home saying, "Reid does not play well with others."

"Is he your alpha? I'm not sure how werewolf politics or whatnot works," I decided to ask.

He scoffed, "No, Mitch is not my alpha. I don't have an alpha. I am what's referred to as a lone wolf."

"Why? I mean, if I could be with my own kind and learn and grow in my power without being a lab rat I would be sorely tempted to do so."

"It's not like that with weres. We are territorial. We have a temper. And that's in human form. Packs protect each other, but they also live under the rule of the alpha." He gave me a predatory smile that should have scared me, but it only made things low in my belly tighten. *Treacherous body!*

He continued with a lower, more controlled tone, "And I, Ms. Delaney, do not play well with others." *Definitely not.*

I swallowed as a rush of heat headed south without any consultation from my brain. He narrowed his eyes and gave me a smile that said he knew what just happened to me. How? Wait, there's no way. Right? I dismissed the thought because I simply did not want to think this man had some way of knowing I was getting a wee bit hot and bothered.

I picked up a file and started paging through it. This witch's name was Holly Franklyn. She was from Atlanta and she was twenty-four. God, she was younger than me. I flipped past the pictures of her ravaged body to a photo of her face. She had beautiful blue eyes and a round face. Her chocolate hair made her blue eyes appear even bluer. She seemed to have some extra weight on her, but on her frame, it looked right. She was an Air witch. Wow, and she was a fairly powerful one based on the two-year-old report from the Coven.

"Did you know this Holly girl was registered? Well, she was two years ago," I asked.

"Yeah, there's a report that the Coven included about her in there," he replied as he shuffled through a file of his own.

"Did you see the rank they gave her power? A freaking eight." He looked at me, confused. I sighed and continued, "Okay, when a witch registers as an adult at the age of eighteen, their power is tested on a scale of one to ten. The members of the Coven's inner circle are all eights to tens. The majority of witches are a three, maybe four. This girl was an eight! I'm surprised she wasn't recruited by the Coven."

He just sat there looking at me. I glanced around and said, "What?"

"I didn't know an eight was a huge deal."

"Oh yeah. Anything above a seven is huge. Sierra was a solid seven, maybe even an eight."

"Okay, I know all of these women were at one point registered, but did not renew. Let's find their ranks."

My heart was pounding. Sierra, seven; Holly, eight; Sarah Ann, seven; Gayle, seven; Grace, eight; Nicole, seven; Marie, eight; Lindsey, seven; Fatima, seven.

"Holy shit, Reid, none of them were under a seven." I looked at him. "How could you have not seen this?"

He glared at me sharply. "I had, but I didn't realize what it meant or even that it was that important." He honestly

65

looked distraught at this revelation. "So, if they were that powerful, why didn't any of them fight back?"

He clearly wasn't a woman. Well, mentally anyway, because physically no one in their right mind could confuse him for anything other than male. There is only one reason they wouldn't have fought back. "Because they knew their attacker and I'm betting they liked him. You know, like romantically."

He just stared at me. Okay, it was just unnerving when he did that. "What? Why do you keep looking at me like that?"

"Nothing, I just keep getting surprised by you." He gave me a slight smile, a slight tilt of his mouth. And just like that heat rushed first to my face then was on its way south when something else caught my eye.

"Bleach? Why were the bodies covered in bleach?" I had to get it together.

"Werewolves can smell all kinds of things," he stated matter-of-factly.

"Okay, like what?"

He moved closer and said, "Every person has a scent. One that is unique to them. And the killer used the bleach to mask any scent he may have left on the bodies. That's why I am an effective investigator. I can also smell emotions if they are strong enough." He gave me a wicked smile and with that I got it. He could smell when I was aroused. My damn body betrayed me. Heat flooded my face. God, I was embarrassed. I was sure he thought I was some silly little girl.

"What do I smell like?" Before I could think the words fell out of my mouth. *Shit, what is wrong with me?*

He smiled. He held my gaze and leaned toward my neck. My heart began to race and my belly tightened. I felt his nose just under my ear and his lips were feather light on my skin. *Am I on fire?* I just had to be because no being, human or otherwise, should produce as much heat as I was giving off. I felt his hand on the back of my neck pull me in slightly. I knew there was no hiding how much this was affecting me, so I didn't even try. I felt more than heard his intake of breath and stifled a moan. In a low almost growl he said, "Like ozone and gardenias."

My breath caught as I felt him press a slight kiss just under my ear. *Oh God.* His hand turned to a fist in my hair as his face moved to hover just over mine. Did I want this? Did I want him? *Hell fucking yes I do. Whoa, calm down, hot sauce.* My thoughts began to haze as his lips lightly brushed mine as if he were dipping a foot in the water to test the temperature. I bet he could hear my heart pounding.

All of a sudden a loud alarm began blazing from the small hotel nightstand. I jumped in surprise. He didn't move, as what I now recognized was his cell phone, rang again. Saved by the damned bell. Still a bit husky, I cleared my throat as the phone rang for a third time and he still didn't move. "You gonna get that?"

He moved so fast I had to stop myself from pitching forward. "What!" he more than snarled into the phone. "No, Mitch, what's up?" Pause. "Okay, see you tomorrow."

We both just sat there. I was sitting at the foot of the bed and he at the head of the bed near the table.

What had almost happened? His hand on the back of my head fisting my hair, his lips, his breath, they took me to a place I have never been before and, frankly, that place scared the hell out of me. I closed my eyes, trying to will my heart rate down to a more normal pace. Was he upset things went that far? I wasn't. Was I? Damned conflicting emotions.

"Reid—"

"Look."

We spoke at the same time. "You first," I said with a shy smile.

"Look, let's get back to the files," he said in a clipped yet professional tone. I guess he was regretting it. I hope I didn't let the disappointment show on my face.

Five hours of looking at gruesome photos, small printed forms, and yellow highlighter. My eyes were starting to cross, so I closed them and flopped back on the bed, groaning. "Ugh, Reid. I think I'm going blind. I cannot read anymore."

"Yeah, it's late, how about you head home and meet up here tomorrow morning so we can take a look at the last file Mitch is bringing. He said he would be here tomorrow morning."

"Oh yeah, okay. What time?"

"Is ten A.M. okay?"

I got up and smoothed my skirt down, about falling over. He was right in front of me.

"You have got to stop doing that," I said a little breathlessly.

He laughed. "What?"

"Being so damned fast, popping up everywhere. You're going to give me a heart attack!"

He laughed again, and the sound of it made my heart do a little flip-flop. God, my body and I were going to have a little conversation. He looked me in the eyes, those caramel eyes that made me want to fall into them and never come out. I felt his arm snake around my waist.

As his right hand held my chin and brushed my lips with his thumb, he whispered, "No, I don't regret what happened. But I don't want to hurt you and we are too close to the full moon for this to be a good idea right now."

And, just like that, heat pooled between my legs. He smiled. *Bastard.* He stroked my lips with his thumb again and as he did I became acutely aware of the hard length of him pressing against me. Suddenly and without warning he let me go and stepped away from me.

"Goodnight, Delaney. I'll see you tomorrow morning," he said, smiling. And with that I left.

Sleep was so out of the question it might as well have been in another galaxy. I had tried everything at that point. I counted five-hundred-something sheep, I turned on Zumba and worked out. I even tried, with increasing desperation, taking a Tylenol PM. So, here I sat, with my third glass of wine on my balcony that overlooked a thick wooded area. One would think the woods would smell of pine and growing green things. Well, in Savannah everything smelled like the marsh.

Reid. Good lord that man was so, so, *male*. Just simply being close to him did things to me I didn't really want to admit to myself. My vision had fogged over. I got up, ready to attempt the sleep thing when something caught my attention out of the corner of my eye.

I looked toward the wooded area. It was really only fifty or so yards away. Now, it could have been my alcohol-flooded perception, but the trees were swirling and there were two small lights peering at me through the moving mass. Were those eyes? Reflecting light? God, how drunk was I?

I shook my head to try to clear the cobwebs that seemed to set in. When I looked again the trees were still trying to tie-dye the night's sky, but the small lights were gone. I set the wine glass down because clearly I was seeing things. I went to bed and this time everything blissfully faded to black.

Running. I was always running. I was so much faster this way. The scenery was a blur. How was I able to run this fast without going ass over foot? God, running like this was freeing, or it would be if I wasn't always being chased.

It was gaining on me. I had to keep running. If whatever was chasing me got me, I knew it would kill me. My heart wasn't just a drum. Well, not just any drum, but a drum solo from a rock concert. A blur of black streaked from my left, landing in front of me. I had to dart to the far right to dodge it. But, in doing so, I didn't see the root of a large, live oak tree sticking out of the ground. My ass went flying over the ground and I rolled into a small grass-covered clearing. I heard what sounded like small soft footfalls coming toward me.

I shook my head to clear it and got up. If I was going to die, I was going to see who the hell was killing me. My brain could not process what my eyes were seeing. Before me stood an impossibly large wolf. It was so black it was almost blue. The moonlight gleamed off its dark pelt, making it seem less like fur and more like polished ebony.

It was snarling and growling at me. Spittle flew from its jaws as it snapped its teeth at me. My heart beat like a wild thing. I brought forth my lightning, pulling it directly from my core and focusing it to my hands. But, when I looked down toward my hands, they weren't there. I saw white paws. Coming from the paws were sparks. From what I could see of the rest of my body, sparks were flying over all of me.

I shifted my gaze to the dark wolf in front of me. And I swear if a wolf's eyes could widen, its eyes did. Waves of some scent hit me. Finally, I knew what the sour scent I had smelled was. It was fear. But, for once it wasn't my fear. A shift in the woods behind the wolf drew my briefest attention. There stood the silhouette of a man. A man I have known since I was a child. He never spoke in my dreams. He would chase me or just watch me, but he was always there.

I sat straight up in bed, my clothes smoked and once again Swiss cheesed. The air reeked of burnt feathers and ozone. I plopped back in bed, too exhausted to even deal with the weirdness that was that dream.

IT WAS 9:50 A.M. AND I SAT IN MY HOT-AS-HELL POS, like the coward I was. *Goddamn it, Delaney.* I had to get my body, brain, and heart all on the same damned page because right now my body was on a whole other damned book. *I can do this,* I chanted in my head.

I opened the door just as my cell began to buzz. Crap, where was that damn phone? I could never keep up with that stupid thing. The display read *Mil.*

"Hey, Mil, I can't…"

"Aye, Laney girl, I need to see you."

"Oh, well hello to you too, Mil. Okay, um, it might not be today, but…"

"Laney girl, it need be today. It's of utter importance."

Utter importance? Okay, Mil never used words like

that. If I said no she would call me every hour on the hour until I caved in.

"Mil, I'm busy right now, but how about I try to make it for dinner?"

"That will do fine. And, girl, you stay out of trouble. My bones tell me you're in a way of it."

"Okay, Mill, I..." I trailed off because the crazy woman hung up.

Mil, other than being my great aunt and the one who raised me, was also one of the most powerful Earth witches I had ever known to live outside the Coven. The Coven had been trying to recruit Mil for as long as I could remember. She would always tell me that she didn't do my cause any favors. She always feared she would draw the attention of the Coven to her and then to me. So, we moved just about every nine months to every year. Mil was used to ruling my life with an iron fist. So, she was more than a little displeased with me when I refused to move again after we settled in Savannah. I sighed audibly. Mil may be a hard ass, but the old hag loved me and she was the only family I had.

I clicked my cell phone; the time read 9:55 A.M. I couldn't put off seeing him anymore. I dressed down today just so I wouldn't tempt him at all. I wore my most worn blue jeans. They hung a little too low on my waist for my taste, but it was the best I could do. I paired them with my old painted-in-several-times, snug-fitting Beatles T-shirt. I had my shoulder-length brown hair tied back in a messy knot and not a lick of makeup on. Well, not counting mascara, because that's not really makeup in my book. I was about a C-cup with a fairly slim waist so playing down my chest was more of a task than I was capable of completing.

I checked my phone again. 9:58 A.M. *Okay, enough procrastinating,* I told myself.

I knocked on the door and braced myself for pure heat. Instead, frost seemed to answer the door. I rocked back on my heels to see if I had the correct hotel room. Yeah, I did. *What the crap is this guy?* The man standing in the doorway was about six foot tall. He had black suit pants on that hid a narrow waist and an ass to die for. Well, what I could see anyway. Tucked into the nice suit pants was a white button down that, thank the gods, had been left open.

My eyes moved from his waist to his chest that was pleasantly bare. This guy could have been ripped from a Calvin Klein ad, and not one with clothes. He had a beautifully sculpted six pack and a chest and shoulders that only dedication could create. His skin was honey colored, almost sun kissed. This man's body had to have been created by Michelangelo. Even his face had hard lines. A full mouth was set in a strong jaw. That was offset by a nose that was borderline too big for his face. His eyes were a vivid green with black flecks. They reminded me of a sliced kiwi. His hair, the color of obsidian, was cut short and obviously wet. If there was a God I would have the wrong room because dealing with two guys as good looking as these two was just mean.

His mouth twitched.

"You must be Delaney," the attractive man said in a deep yet smooth voice.

I hung my head and mumbled, "There is no God."

I mean, for real. Two men in one room who both looked like they stepped right out of a workout ad, that's just not right. If there is a God, he's clearly sadistic and enjoying himself immensely at my expense.

"What?" he said, clearly having heard me if the smile playing at the corners of his mouth had anything to say about it. Great, the cosmos were just lovin' on me today.

"Oh nothing, you must be Mitch."

"I am indeed, Delaney." When he shook my hand I didn't feel the pure heat like I did with Reid. With Mitch it was almost frosty, which was weird because the lust was palpable. Oddly enough the lust wasn't mine.

"Delaney, hey!" Reid called.

From my limited view, I saw Reid stop short and glare at the back of Mitch's head. If Reid's eyes had been lasers, they would have bored twin holes right through his skull. "Mitch, could you put a shirt on or close the one you have?" he all but growled.

Mitch let his eyes travel down the length of my body, hesitating on my breasts. What was that saying? Oh, that's right, he undressed me with his eyes. Well, that's what it felt like he did and frankly it was unnerving. Waiting a fraction of a second more than was polite, he then smiled and raked his eyes over me once more before saying, "Sure thing, boss." That last word he spat.

Reid and I walked out to the parking lot while we waited on Mitch to get fully dressed. Much to my great disappointment.

"Well, Mitch seems ... nice." God was my face flushed? Lord, these men are going to be the death of me.

"Yeah, something like that," Reid muttered.

REID JAMISON

SIX

I REALLY HATED THAT DELANEY WAS IN THE MIDDLE OF this, but there wasn't much I could do at this point. I had to take her to the crime scene. I needed to see if she found anything there that she recognized that belonged to Sierra.

If Mitch wasn't a good friend and if I hadn't worked with him before, I might rip the bastard's throat out for how he looked at Delaney. And did the bastard think me a new pup without a sense of smell? The lust wafted off of him like waves in the damned sea. I bet Delaney could smell it.

Let's be realistic about this. She's not mine and I have no claim on her. *Then why the hell do I feel so territorial over her? Ah, fuck me.* Two territorial males with an unclaimed female. Today was going to test my willpower.

"Mitch, we need to talk about Delaney," I said on the short drive to President Street. We needed to set some kind of ground rules. Delaney was following us in her car.

As she said, my Jeep looked a bit small for the three of us. She wasn't stupid and I had to quit underestimating her. She knew damn well something was brewing between Mitch and me.

Mitch grunted in the affirmative. "I assume there's an attraction to her?" he questioned.

"Uh, yeah." Why couldn't Delaney be less than she was? It would make my life easier.

"And I guessing neither of us want to put a claim on her?" Mitch questioned.

When a werewolf puts a claim on an unclaimed female, it's like saying back off, she's owned property. Claiming a female was not permanent like a mating was, but mating can only happen with another werewolf. Claiming doesn't take the urge of an unmated female away, but it helps ease the tension between unmated males. Though, it's more like the were/human/witch version of marriage, and mating I would say is so much more than marriage. It goes beyond death. You're mated until you both die, and if one dies, typically the other will soon follow.

Mating between weres is like the combining of souls. What were two became one. It is said that the souls are together even after death. The first and last female I claimed was my wife when I was first turned. I never had the chance to turn her so we could mate. I killed her before we could.

"No, that's out of the question," I told him.

"I agree, we are here for a job and Delaney can't be part

of it. In fact, we need to get her out of this investigation altogether. Why is she here? Hot piece of ass she may be, she's going to cause problems." He emphasized the word *ass* and it made me want to throttle him. I proceeded to roll the window down. I had to empty this Jeep of the built-up testosterone; it was getting so thick I was about to choke. As soon as the window was down, the tension in the car eased markedly.

"Sierra was her only friend and she just showed up at the police station. Honestly, I don't want her to go out on her own for some damn vengeance quest. We need to get this son of a bitch. I don't want her blood on my hands." *Like Beth's,* I didn't say.

"I agree. But for now we can't take our actions personally; it's in our nature. Let's just get through this without ruining our friendship and killing each other."

I'd known Mitch going on twenty years. There's always been something I haven't trusted about him, but that stems from us both having alpha tendencies, and me not acting on them. Mitch had helped me in the past and we have remained friendly because of the sheer fact that we leave each other alone. I respect how he has handled his pack in Atlanta, so I really have no bone to pick with him. He knew what happened with Beth and never brought it up, so for that alone I held a good deal of respect for the man.

Mitch always embraced what we were. He denied his inner beast nothing. So, if he wanted Delaney, he would not hesitate in taking her, as long as she was willing. But, if he went after Delaney, I didn't think I couldn't stop myself from ripping his jugular out. Surely just a flesh wound, something he would heal from, but I didn't want to let it get to that point. I had an image of an armless knight stating, "It was just a flesh wound." I have a morbid sense of humor sometimes. Stifling the thought, I focused on the present. I would not claim her. I would not sentence to her the same fate as Beth.

Finally I said, "Agreed."

SIERRA'S BODY WAS FOUND JUST EAST OF RIVER STREET near the railroad tracks on President Street. It seemed a homeless person saw a naked man covered in blood. The homeless man got spooked at the sight and ran off to call police. Apparently, there was a homeless camp not too far from where the body was discovered.

She was attacked about thirty yards away from the river and then dragged through the brush toward the street and to the railroad tracks, based on the police report. The police made this more difficult by not doing much of the investigating. Once they learned a victim was a witch, they called a representative from the Coven and got the body out of their metaphorical hair. Witches were easily identified after death because their eyes turned white as soon as the life left their body. When a human dies, their pupils may dilate, but they stay somewhat normal, for a few days anyway.

Sierra's apartment wasn't but a mile or two away, but the nagging question was why she was here in the first place. From the photos of the body, she had been mauled to the point of death. Her body was found on the full moon, whereas the other bodies were dumped on the new moon. *Why the change?* It seemed there was a werewolf who was trying to change a witch, but why? It's common knowledge that changing a witch is impossible. Someone had to have seen something that caused the wolf to leave the body here and not take it with him and see if she rose. Which was impossible. This whole thing made no sense.

The three of us walked the area in silence for about two hours until we found our way to the bank of the river.

"Why in the world would anyone be down here?" Mitch said.

I honestly had no idea why anyone would come over here, as the only thing this place had going for it was that it was secluded. So, I shrugged at his question. The river wasn't very scenic and it was disgusting with all of the grime of the city upriver. River Street itself was fairly well maintained due to it and the city being a heavy tourist attraction, but this place didn't even seem like locals would go here. The thought must have projected on my face because Delaney spoke.

"We are unregistered witches. We like to be close to our element. It's not like Serra could go sit on the water in the middle of the river. This place is only a few miles from her apartment. No one would ever come here. That's the point. That's why she came here. As unregistered witches, we are hiding from the human government that will force us to register and move on their reservations and the Coven, who is essentially doing the same thing."

"Why don't you just register? I mean, it seems like the easy choice to me," Mitch asked and I did wonder a similar question. I knew with Delaney's powers she would be much like a laboratory rat; that is, if she was lucky. Or they would use her for their own deluded purposes, her morals be damned.

She walked right up to Mitch and looked up at him in challenge while she said in a steady voice, "Because, Mitch, I do not want to live a semi-life. A life ruled by the Coven and ruled by humans. Humans wish us gone or dead and the Coven wants to use us to further their own agenda. When they are done with us all that would be left would be our bones and I, Mitch, am much more than bones."

She turned to walk away when Mitch asked, "What's your power, little witch?"

Walking toward me, she stopped and said over her shoulder, "Earth. But, I'm not near as powerful as Sierra was."

In the span of about ten seconds we had a wordless conversation all in body language.

"Liar."

"I don't tell anyone. I don't have to."

"I won't tell, but I don't think Mitch will either."

"Drop it."

Her face was flushed with emotion. She was getting frazzled and it was turning her face a beautiful shade of pink. The male in me wanted to push the issue, but I would let it drop, for now.

"Okay, Reid, you want to change or do you want me to? We need to walk the path the body was drug. There are some questions we need to answer."

Delaney's eyes met mine as I smiled my best predatory smile and said, "I will."

Changing from human to werewolf was a shape shift. It only took about five or so minutes outside of the full moon. On the full moon, the process only took about two minutes, but no matter the amount of time, the process was agonizingly painful. A wolf was at their most powerful at the apex of the full moon and at their weakest at the apex of the new moon. I'd heard that a were is drained of power to help raise a new wolf. But, I have never made a wolf so I didn't know how true that was.

I found a somewhat private place and began stripping my clothes off. While the idea of being naked with Delaney was quite appealing, Mitch being here was unappealing, to say the least. Stripping was a necessary part of the change, as I didn't need shredded clothes. I closed my eyes and focused on the change. I took a deep breath and called it forward, allowing the wolf's essence to take me over.

Skin ripped and then healed with fur, bones broke and reformed into a new inhuman shape. The pain was near maddening. Every bone that breaks is white hot. Every reformation of my skin and limbs felt like acid being poured over my whole body. The wolf I keep at bay as a human stretched its legs, readying itself to take control, but I never let it get the upper hand. Scents bombarded me and sounds temporarily deafened me. In our human form we have heightened senses, but in wolf form, they are heightened one hundred fold.

I shook my head, flopping my ears, trying to shake off the pins-and-needles feeling covering my skin. In my wolf form I was a tawny color with black specks on the tips of my fur. Like most weres, I sport electric-green eyes. We are not wolves, nor are we human. We do have a human nature, as well as a wolf's. This was a difficult concept to grasp when I was first changed.

I made my way back to Delaney and Mitch. My hackles rose at the scent of Mitch. *He's not your alpha,* I told myself. I smelled her long before I saw her. Ozone and gardenias, Delaney's scent. I paused for just a moment, breathing her in. She had dressed down today, but oh god she was beautiful. She had her back to me. I walked up to her and her back stiffened and she slowly turned around.

Her eyes widened and she took a few good steps back. I wanted to jump on her. Rip her apart. My mouth began to water, causing me to pant. No, not rip her apart. I wanted to jump on her for other things. And the scary part was my wolf agreed.

"Delaney, stop. Don't move. It's still Reid, but he's trying to get control and your fear smells good. Don't back away. Remember, you're not prey, so don't act like it."

I tiled my head at him as if to say, *"I would never hurt her, you moron."*

Delaney took a few deep breaths, causing my eyes to settle on her beautifully sculpted breasts. This wasn't helping me not want her. *This is a job.*

"Wow, he's huge. He's got to be five feet tall!" she said, smiling. "Can I touch him?"

"Let him come to you," Mitch replied.

I walked up to her. I wanted nothing more than to feel her fingers in my fur. At my full height I was indeed about 5' from head to paws. Delaney was about 5'5 so I almost came up to her eye level. I ducked my head and put my nose in her belly, snuffling and nuzzling her. She giggled.

"Hey!" she said as she pushed my head slightly. "God, you are the most beautiful thing I have ever seen." She ran delicate fingers through the fur at the back of my ears. That's when it hit me. Even as this beast she still lusted after me.

"Okay, enough play time. We have work to do," Mitch growled.

I guessed he could sense it too. I nodded and walked over to Mitch.

I breathed in the scents, trying to find the metallic scent of blood on the air. Blood, even if it had been spilled days ago, tended to linger in dirt. I smelled squirrels and raccoons, but no blood. I widened my perimeter and then found it. It was about ten yards away from the river in a densely wooded area.

I sat down and barked once. Shortly, Mitch and Delaney came toward me. Delaney walked right up next to me and placed her hand on my head. It was a possessive touch and made me happy, even though it shouldn't. I ducked my head, breaking the contact, and sniffed around, then began to follow the trail.

"Wait, where is he going?" Delaney exclaimed.

"This is where she was killed. He's showing us the trail the killer took while dragging the body."

"Oh, can y'all communicate telepathically?"

Mitch laughed. "No, but I know Reid enough to know what he's doing and I know body language."

I sat down and waited for them to catch up. This spot seemed to smell stronger of blood than most. Just before I went on, I saw Mitch put his hand on the small of her back to lead her forward. At that moment I don't think I had ever wanted to rip someone's throat out more. I met his eyes and he met mine. The contact was enough to have me taking a step forward.

He moved his hand and said in a low tone, "Not now, and I'm sorry."

Delaney's eyes flicked from me and then to Mitch. I shook my head and returned to the trail. The trail started out with little brush, then the trees, bushes, and shrubbery began to get thick and difficult to maneuver even in wolf form.

"Ouch! Shit, there are huge thorns everywhere," I heard Delaney say several paces behind me.

There was no way a wolf could drag a body through here without changing. The brush was too damned thick. About fifteen minutes later we got to the railroad tracks and about a hundred yards from the road the trail stopped. I sat on the spot for a few beats waiting on Mitch and Delaney. I looked at Mitch. He nodded and handed me my clothes in a backpack. I walked over, but when I did I caught the scent of fresh blood. I sniffed the air then looked at Delaney. She was cut somewhere.

I walked over to her and saw a small cut on her inner right arm. I sniffed it when she said, "Oh, oops. Damned thorns..." she trailed off as I licked the wound. The taste of her blood alone showed me I could not trust myself alone with this girl. Her blood tasted like a human's, but it sizzled with power. I turned toward my things, grasped them in my teeth, and walked off. The wolf was getting the upper hand so I needed to change. Right damn now.

"Okay," I said, clearing my throat. Clearly, I surprised Delaney because at the sound her shoulders jerked in surprise.

"I swear to God, you have got to stop doing that," she

said a little breathlessly. When her voice sounded like that it made my cock twitch. Okay? brute, calm down.

"Sorry, but having just walked that trail there's no way a wolf could have drug a body through all of those obstacles and brush. He had to have shifted to do it," I said with complete confidence. Without opposable thumbs, trying to drag a body through all of this forestry would have been near impossible.

"That was my thought too. There was a 911 caller. The files said a homeless man called and reported a naked man covered in blood. And when they arrived they found the body," Mitch said.

"Sierra."

We both turned to Delaney and looked at her.

"What?" Mitch said, breaking the silence.

"Her name was Sierra. Not the body, not the victim, and you will not dehumanize her. Even if she was a witch," Delaney said calmly, even though it was clear by the flush in her face that she was anything but calm.

Before I could say something, Mitch said, "Delaney, it's not personal." As soon as the words left his mouth I wanted to throttle him.

Delaney seemed to vibrate. The scent of ozone grew and I knew in this moment there was danger with her. I didn't know if I should be a bit afraid or, my personal morals be damned, if I should claim her right there on the ground for Mitch and God to see.

"Oh, Mitch. Yes, it's very personal. This THING came into my life. It killed the closest thing I had to a sister. You can't get more personal than that. You don't have to like me, or the fact that I'm here, but, Mitch, I will find a way to get justice for Sierra. You can count on that." For a second I saw lightning behind Delaney's eyes, but it was gone so fast I couldn't be sure I saw anything there.

"Delaney, I'm sorry. We will be sure to be a little better about referring to her," I said, trying to defuse the situation. Not only because she could fry both of us to beef jerky before we could lick our balls, but because she looked as though she were in pain. The thought that she was hurting because of something I did and could have avoided killed me inside. I realized that I would do just about anything to never cause her pain and to always alleviate any ache she felt. *Shit, this female is breaking so many of my rules.*

"I'm sorry, Delaney," Mitch said.

There was a moment of awkward silence and tension.

"There is a homeless camp not far from here. We should go find the guy who called 911," Delaney replied, breaking the tension.

"There is? Where?" Mitch said.

Hell, I didn't know about the camp.

"Yeah, it's just under the Truman overpass. It's really only something you would know if you were a local. But, it proves that this guy wasn't a local. I mean, if you knew there were a camp of homeless people just on the other side of the tracks, would you kill someone? I mean, they could come up on you at any time. Just like we think happened here."

I think we both just gaped at her. Lord, this woman just kept surprising me. I glanced over at Mitch and he looked as dumbfounded as I felt.

"What?" she asked, placing her hand on her shapely hips. She then began to tap her right foot at us as if to say, *come on, you stupid men, get with it*. At that moment I felt like a stupid man.

"We guessed he wasn't local, but you sure put the nail in the coffin," I said.

"What was the homeless man's name?" Delaney asked.

"Cowboy Bill," Mitch stated.

"Who has a name like Cowboy Bill? I bet his real name is Steve."

I raised my eyebrow at Delaney and said, "Then wouldn't his name be Cowboy Steve?"

She chuckled and said, "Shut up."

After four or so hours of looking in the homeless camp for Cowboy Bill, we called it quits and went back to the hotel. However, during our trip to the oh-so-wonderful homeless camp, we did learn a few things about the infamous Cowboy Bill.

Cowboy Bill, or Billy Boy, was not local to Savannah. He came to Savannah in the colder months and left in the summer months. However, he had been doing some odd jobs getting some cash so he had stuck around this summer. According to several of the homeless, Cowboy Bill was a big-time drinker and small-time drug user. Oh, and the small fact that he was crazy. Bill was, as one person said, "A tall-tail tellin' fool."

After he stumbled upon the bloody man and body, he became paranoid and withdrew from his friends and associates. No one had seen him all day, but nonetheless, we left our cards to have him call us. *Yeah, like that will ever happen.* We got back to the hotel around 4 P.M.

"Delaney, want to go back out to the homeless camp again tomorrow? Mitch is going to see the … Sierra's body, and see what he can find out there." Her answers never mattered before, but for some reason they did now.

She smiled brightly and said, "Sure, see you at ten."

I turned and walked away just so she wouldn't see my smile in return.

DELANEY HAGEN
SEVEN

REID IN HIS WOLF FORM WAS THE MOST AMAZING thing I had ever seen. His coat was a tawny color with specks of black, the feel of it like silk. He resembled a normal timber wolf, but a hell of a lot bigger. He was only a few inches shorter than me in his wolf form. His eyes were electric green and still sparked with his humanity. And when he licked me, sweet God I about passed out from the speed of my wild heart beat alone.

I glanced at the time on the dash; it read 4:10. Great, that gave me time to get home, shower, and get to Mil's. I turned the key and heard a big bunch of nothing. *Ugh,* I groaned. *Really? Not this again.* I not so softly banged my head on the steering wheel. *Could this day get any worse?* Well there it was, I thought it so now it's going to happen. I tried the key again. The car sputtered and died. Well, at least it didn't explode. That was something positive, wasn't it?

I heard a brisk knock at my window. I jumped at the noise, then looked up and was met with Reid's hot caramel gaze. I licked my lips. Oh God, did I really just do that? His eyes dropped to my lips and his eyebrows went up in question. I felt my face began to warm with flush.

I cracked the door and said, "It's dead. I guess I'll need to call a friend or a c-"

"Stop, Delaney. I'll take you home." Oh, because him and me alone was a great idea. I would just tell him thanks but no thanks.

"Yeah, okay thanks," I blurted. Apparently, my hormones controlled my mouth. *Damned hormones.*

He opened my door, but when I got out he didn't give me that much space so our bodies brushed, sending a spike of heat to my core. *He cannot be this close to me. My brain gets all fuzzy when he's this close to me.* All I could think about were his hands all over me. His lips and tongue. *Okay, listen, hot sauce, you need to calm down.* I took a deep breath and met that hot caramel gaze again.

"Uh o-okay, let's go."

He smiled and said, "Yes, let's."

After I sat down in the Jeep, I pulled out my cell and texted my friend Troy. Troy was a friend Sierra and I met one night when we went to Club One, the local gay bar. When we met Troy, he was bartending. He was wearing a long white toga with gold and purple ribbons trailing down his arms and a gold belt cinching his waist, which, by the way, was impossibly tiny. His bust was sloshing out of his top and I always wondered how he managed to get them to look so real! Hell, I had a hard time not staring at them. I swear to God he had to use Jell-O molds to make his boobs look so real because there's just no way. His long black hair was swept up into a braid that wrapped around his head, looking much like a crown, with gold leaves sticking out of it. Over his left, um, breast? Pec? His nametag read *Helen of Troy.*

The best way to describe Troy would be "a male peacock." Troy sure did love his feathers. Troy in drag was a better-looking woman than I was. I couldn't help but be a tiny bit jealous of him, with his smooth, light-coffee-colored skin and hazel eyes that definitely made you look twice. From our first meeting at the bar on, Troy had adopted Sierra and me as his sisters. Or, as Troy put it, "Y'all are my sisters from other misters. Well, I guess we could be the same daddy because my daddy was white and from how I hear it, that mother fucker, pun absolutely intended, got around."

I typed in:

Hey want to go see Mil with me? I need a ride my car died.

Troy:

Again?! Yeah you know I'll go. My hair is in the bathtub drying. Some hooker tossed a bloody Mary at me. Bitch better not have ruined my new wig. What time?

Me:

6? Get there at 7? She's cooking!

Troy:

Okay. Glad you told me. I'll bring my big girl panties.

I shook my head at the screen. If nothing else, Troy was entertaining.

"You ready?" Reid asked.

"Oh yeah, sorry. I was just texting a friend."

Reid raised his eyebrows at me and I didn't answer his implied question. He put the car in drive and drove to my apartment.

My apartment was only a few miles from the hotel and I could have run to it, but it was hot. Really damned hot.

"Hey, look, thanks for the ride. I guess I'll call someone to come tow the car. I will just run to the hotel in the morning."

"No, I'll pick you up," he said as he pulled the Jeep into a parking space at the entrance of the stairs leading up to my apartment.

Okay just get out of the car, go upstairs, and get out of an enclosed space with this male.

"Want to come up for coffee?" *Did I just say that? Did those words just come out of my mouth?* My hormones really were taking over. *Please say no.* Wait, did I really want him to say no? I was so conflicted when it came to this male.

"Sure," he said, smiling. I think he knew my head and hormones were involved in a civil war.

"I thought we could talk about the case and what we are going to do from here," I hastily added.

Coffee was my weakness, always had been. I'd drink it 24/7 if I didn't need to sleep. Right now, my hands were shaking making the stuff. This man had me turning into some twitty little chick, but I would not fall over him like a crazy woman. That's all there was to it.

I handed him his coffee and sat down next to him. God, just being next to him made heat rush to places I really wished it wouldn't.

"So, what do we do now? I mean, until we can find Cowboy Bill?"

"Well, Mitch is going to the morgue tomorrow. Delaney, this guy has been very careful. He uses bleach on the bodies and in his tracks so we can't scent him. And even when there is no bleach I still can't scent him. I think the best thing we can do is find his motive and try to predict his next move." Reid looked frustrated; hell, I felt frustrated.

"The Coven has no ideas? I mean, I question why they care again."

"Well, logically they don't want the press making a big deal of a bunch of witches dying. Even though a lot of humans fear witches, there are witch sympathizing groups and they could cause the Coven a lot of issues."

"When have you known the Coven to be logical when there's no profit in it for them?"

Reid seemed to think about this question. Good, he should be thinking about it because the Coven is a group of corrupt old bastards and bitches. They care about the inner circle of the Coven and everyone else be damned.

"I did ask the Coven why they were involved in this and they said the why of it was just as I told you, but if I'm being honest with you, they do seem to have an endgame that I can't quite figure out."

"I think going to the Coven is your next step. Or getting someone who wants to rat on the Coven."

"That's not a bad idea," he said as he reached his impossibly large hand out to my face. I stiffened as he brushed a small strand of hair that worked its way loose from my mess of a bun thing that sat atop my head. His touch made my heart beat so fast I could have been related to a hummingbird. And it made things low in my belly tighten.

He had a wicked smile on his face.

"What?" I said, my voice a little too husky for my taste.

"I need to tell you. I can smell you."

Oh my god. I showered and put deodorant on. I was purely mortified. I turned red and I think he saw the pure panic on my face because he moved his hand to the back of my head and chuckled low in his chest.

"No, I mean I can smell you when you're aroused. I can smell when you want me."

I just stared at him, dumbfounded. I mean, what does one say to that?

"Um okay, I—" I was cut off when he leaned forward and covered my mouth with his.

His mouth was so warm on mine. The kiss was feather

light at first, a question he was giving me time to respond to. I leaned closer to him, deepening the kiss. His tongue flicked my bottom lip before he sucked it in his mouth. Heat rushed from the hand tangled in my hair to my core and began to pool. He pushed the kiss even closer to the edge as his tongue began a more sensual assault of my mouth. I pressed myself closer to him, pushing my breasts against his too-warm chest. The warmth of his skin through his shirt and mine left my breasts needing to be touched, and my nipples tingling. I needed him to touch me.

As if he heard my thoughts, he broke our kiss and moved his hands to my ass, lifting me up onto his lap. I opened my legs to straddle him, pressing my core against his hard length. I groaned at the feel of him. Somewhere deep down I knew there was a thought I should be having. It was important, but as soon as I had the thought it was chased away by his hand at the back of my head, grasping my hair and lifting my head back as he began to suck lightly on my throat.

I gasped and dug my nails into his back. He grunted at me and then bit, causing me to squeak in surprise and delight. I felt his other hand snake its way under my shirt. I drew in a quick, much-needed gulp of air as his hands made a trail of heat across my skin. He cupped my left breast and quickly found the nipple through my bra, rolling the pebbled flesh between his finger and thumb. Just like that, all thoughts about anything other than Reid were ejected right out my head.

Suddenly he released me and pushed me back on the couch. I looked up at him, confused. What had happened? He was right there with me, wasn't he?

"Take it off, Delaney, or I'm going to rip it off." It was a demand, not a polite question. His voice was guttural and raw, laced with need. I took my shirt off and he did the same. God, the sight of him without a shirt on was enough to bring me to climax.

I began to throb in my most sensitive of places. He had my bra off and me pushed back on the couch before I could even react to him moving. He was fast, but this time I didn't mind a bit. He loomed over me, taking in the sight of my body. It honestly made me feel self-conscious to have a man as beautiful as him looking at me with such fierceness and lust on his face. He licked his lips and lowered himself atop me. His hand cupped my breast and our eyes met for the briefest of moments. His eyes blazed with green and mine, I knew, had lightning in them.

He smiled and dipped his head to my breast, drawing my nipple into his mouth painfully slowly. I felt his right hand slip under my ass and he lifted me even closer to him. He aligned us, pelvis to pelvis, and I groaned as his erection was ground against me, somehow finding my clit though all of our remaining clothes. His thrusts sent electricity through my body. I moaned out loud.

He withdrew my nipple from his mouth and said huskily, "Every time I touch you, your skin gives off a charge, and God it's the hottest thing I have ever felt. You're like touching a live wire."

Before I had time to process anything he said, he lowered his head to my left breast and began to flick my nipple with his tongue. He drew it in his mouth, sucking gently at first, then suddenly he bit down sharply, causing me to cry out in pleasure.

My brain was mush. I slid my right hand down his chest and his breath caught. My fingers came to the waistband of his pants and I slipped my hand in. His eyes met mine as my hand dipped lower and I wrapped my fingers around his oh-so-large erection. Oh my, there was no way he would fit. It was so hot, it felt like lava poured through his veins. His eyes closed as I grasped him and he groaned, pushing his hips more fully into my hand. How was this man going to fit inside me? Just the thought of him inside me set me on fire.

Knock, knock, knock. The sound was muffled. It sounded like someone was knocking at the damned door.

"Girl, open the fucking door. My wig fell in the bathtub and now it's clogged. I can't take a shower in those conditions. I have standards."

Troy's voice seemed to reverberate through my tiny apartment. Talk about cold water. For what seemed to be hours we both just lay there staring at each other.

"DE-Lane-E, girl come on, you're leaving me standing out here lookin' like a hot damn mess. If I miss out on a good man, girl…"

"I'm coming, one second!" I yelled to Troy. God knew he would just keep talking and my neighbors would really get an earful. I moved my hand from Reid's pants and went to get off of him and find my shirt. As I went to move he grabbed my shoulders and kept an iron grip on them. What was he doing? Troy was all about making a scene. I had to get that queen in the apartment before he had a fit of epic proportions.

"Delaney, look at me," Reid said in a low and very controlled tone. It was a tone that demanded action be taken and god help you if it wasn't the correct one. I looked at his blazing green eyes. "Delaney, we will finish this. This won't be something I will let you forget or regret. I don't want to be drawn to you, but I am, and I know you're drawn to me."

I was breathless, mainly because he was right. I was drawn to him even though I didn't want to be.

He leaned closer until our noses were almost touching. My breathing became ragged. Just being close to him like this had my body aching for his touch and ready for other, more enjoyable activities.

"I can hear you!" Troy bellowed through the door, eliciting a snarl from Reid. "Come on, I—"

"She will be there in a minute!"

Well, that shut Troy right on up.

"I don't think anyone has ever gotten him to shut up so comp…" He moved so fast I couldn't even react other than to take in a gasp of breath. His mouth covered mine and he swallowed whatever words I was going to say. It was a fierce kiss full of promise. When he broke it, I was light-headed and my lips felt swollen, and I knew they were a shade of dusky rose. He slowly brought his lips to my ear, leaving kisses along my jaw. I could hear his ragged breathing and it sent heat throughout my body. *Oh, but I can't; Troy is here, but damn Reid is just so much male.*

Reid drew in a breath and whispered low, "I want to be inside you."

I stopped breathing. My heart began racing like a wild thing. *Wasn't there someone I needed to be thinking about?* He drew my earlobe in his mouth and suckled it. *Oh sweet mother of God.*

I gulped air and managed to pant, "Reid, I ... I…"

"You, you what, Delaney?" he said with a low chuckle. What was I going to say? It was important. *Oh fuck it.*

"I don't want you to stop," I said, pushing my naked breasts against his chest. He drew in a sharp breath and made a low growling noise.

"If you keep doing that I won't stop and whoever that is outside is going to have a long wait."

"Oh shit, Troy," I said. God, this man fogged my mind beyond belief. "I, uh, need you to get off me. I need to go let Troy in or he will make a scene."

Reid smiled and nipped me on the nose, then licked my bottom lip. He slowly lifted off and sat astride me. His eyes still blazed green as his gaze slipped from mine to my breasts. My heart rate and breathing increased. A look of fierce hunger flashed across his face. This man did things to me that did not yet have a name!

His eyebrows raised slightly and he looked at me with an expression of challenge. I raised my hands to touch his face, but he caught them in midair. His hands wrapped around my wrists and he pinned them above my head, causing my back to arch and my breasts to jut out toward him. He looked at them as if they were a delicacy he had never been offered before. I swallowed the lump in my throat. His hands were like an iron vice around me. And, oh God be damned, if that wasn't turning me on more. If that was even possible.

"Reid." It came out a scant whisper.

His head dipped to my left breast and he flicked the pebbled flesh with his tongue. He moved and did the same to my right breast.

"Just something to remember me by," he said as he released my hands and eased off of me.

Panting. That man left me aching and panting. I just lay there trying to calm my heart and regulate my breathing. Troy! Crap balls. Where was my bra? *Shit. Damnit, where is that thing?* I found my shirt and tossed it on. Well, let's hope I didn't get cold. I looked up to find Reid buttoning up his shirt. It should be a crime for him to wear clothes at all. Then I had a vision of him causing all kinds of car accidents because others couldn't keep their eyes off of him. *Yeah, maybe not.*

I pulled open the door to find a rather pissy-looking Troy staring back at me. Pissy he may be, but I knew he wanted to see who I had in here as I never had men over. Well, besides Troy. It's not that I had never dated, but with my secrets and the small fact that I could possibly electrocute someone, I just stayed away from men. And the sex thing, well, I have never wanted to try that, until now that is. I had never been attracted to someone enough to risk them finding out about me or hurting them.

Troy's eyes widened and lifted several inches above me and I knew he was looking at Reid. As if I couldn't feel him pressed against me. The heat radiating from his chest to my back made my nipples harden. His hands rested on my shoulders and I didn't think anyone could miss the gesture as being anything but possessive. *This man is just too much.*

A little breathless I said, "T-Troy, this is Reid Jamison. Reid, this is Troy Tipton. He's taking me to see Mil."

"Well. Oh my day-um. Delaney girl, don't we just have things to talk about," Troy said, eyeing Reid. Troy licked his lips and said to Reid, "Hello, tall, dark, and big." I felt myself stiffen at his remark. Troy flirted with anything that moved and was male, but for some reason I wanted to rip him apart for looking at Reid as if he were his next meal. I never heard Reid's laugh. I only felt it in my back.

"Hi, Troy, don't mind me I was just leaving. Nice to

meet you," Reid said with an even tone.

I felt him move from my back and slide sideways through the doorway. My back felt entirely too cold after his warmth was stolen from me. All the while Troy's eyes never left Reid. Was I feeling possessive of Reid? *I need to calm the hell down.* Before Reid got too far from me he leaned down and put his finger under my chin, drawing my face up to his, and kissed me deeply. With that one finger he held up my entire weight. When he ended the kiss we were both a little breathless. And by both, I mean Troy and I. He gave me a cocky smile that said, "That's right, I'm staking my claim." *But, that can't be right. Can it?*

"I'll see you tomorrow, Delaney," he said as he turned and walked down the hallway.

We both stood there, staring at the back of him.

DELANEY HAGEN
EIGHT

"**G**IRL, THAT ASS, THAT BACK . . . YOU BETTER GET your skinny white ass in that apartment and tell me everything. And I mean everything, like the size of his co..."

"Oh my God, Troy! Okay, I'm going," I said, backing into the apartment, holding the door open for him to enter.

Troy entered my tiny apartment and turned to me not five feet from the door. His hands were on his hips and he was leaning on one leg, tapping the other foot as if he were waiting for something.

"What?" I said, giving him a sheepish smile. I walked past Troy to sit down at the small kitchen table, and crossed my arms over my chest. It was at that moment I remembered I did not have a bra on. Ugh, where was that thing. Troy plopped on the couch and yelped.

"What's wrong? Are you okay?"

"Yes. I think one of your springs is busted. It poked me in the ass," he replied, digging in the sofa. His eyes widened then narrowed at me.

"What? Look, I don't want to talk..." I trailed off as he pulled out my bra from the couch. It had been ripped right down the middle and was still clasped in the back. My mouth fell open in shock as heat flamed in my face. I closed my eyes. *When I open my eyes he will not be holding my bra*, I mentally chanted. I opened my eyes and found Troy studying my mangled bra.

"Lucy, you got some 'splaining to do," Troy mocked in his best Cuban accent.

"Ugh, okay. Look, you go take a shower and I clearly need to change and I'll tell you about him on the way to Mil's."

"Okay, but this," he said, holding up my bra high above his head for me to see, "had better be a hell of a story."

I rolled my eyes at him and went to the bedroom to dress.

Mil lived about an hour outside of Savannah proper. She typically refused all things city of any kind. When I was growing up, Mil and I moved every nine months to a year. According to her, it was because she did not want the Coven to find me and use me for my "Ne'er before seen powers."

Mil was a member of the inner circle of the all-powerful Coven. When I was about four years old, she left the Coven to help my mother train me with my newly discovered talents. My mom really had no idea how to handle a child who kept blowing things up and electrocuting the cat. My poor parents were not witches and they had no clue how to keep me from barbecuing our pets and burning down the house, so they called Mil.

Scientists said the gene was random and not hereditary, but I didn't buy that. The "witch gene" did seem to be stronger in our family. Mil would always gloss over the witch origin and say something like, "Ah, what need do you have to know such things?" Only a year or so after Mil came to live with us and left the Coven, my parents died in a car accident. A car accident I caused.

"Okay, girl, you need to spill about Mister Tall, Dark, and Oh My God Sexy!" Troy said as he slipped into the black-and-pink Mini Cooper.

Lord this man just could not wait for answers. I went over how I met Reid and how I interjected myself into Sierra's case. I skipped over our heated encounter in his hotel room and in my apartment.

"God, I miss her, D," Troy said as a tear rolled down his café-latte-colored cheek. I did not want to cry. I put my hand in his, lacing our fingers together. We sat in silence for about thirty minutes.

"Well so what was HE doing in your apartment and why did he kiss you like he was in hell and you were a glass of ice water. And damn, did you see the way he looked at you? Shit, it was intense."

My face must have been a light shade of red because Troy pushed on with his look of, *"Girl, I will not stop asking so give up now."*

I sighed in resignation. "I don't know what to say. He's so overbearing, so male, so, ugh, I don't know. But whatever he is, I am drawn to him like a moth to the proverbial flame. Troy, I can't explain it! I don't want to be attracted to him, but I can't seem to stop myself."

"Does he know that you could possibly electrocute his ass?" Troy quested with an amused look on his face.

Troy had only known about my abilities after some drunk guy started harassing us one night when we were out and I lost my temper. I only ended up giving the guy a slight electrical charge as I slapped him, but it was enough to knock him out for a solid ten seconds and it was enough for Troy to question what I was. When I finally told him he made me call forth my lightning and show him. What was his response? "Holy shit, girl, so you don't have to pay an electric bill? Can you room with me so I don't have to pay one?"

"Yes, he knows. I kind of freaked out when he told me just what he was."

Troy stared at the road ahead of us and asked, "Well, what is he? Now you have to tell me."

"Um a werewolf," I said, the words hidden in a garbled mess as I cleared my throat.

"I'm sorry, what did you say?" Troy replied, never taking

his eyes off the road.

I sighed and said in a resigned tone, "He's a werewolf."

The car suddenly swerved into the oncoming lane. "Troy!" I yelled at him, trying to get him to put the car back into the appropriate lane. With a quick jerk of the wheel the car was back on track.

"Shit, girl, you can't just drop a bomb like that," Troy said, breathing rapidly.

"Sorry."

"But, you did say w-werewolf correct?" Troy asked. Clearly his normal was just stuffed in a rocket and shot to kingdom come. Boy, did I know the feeling. I nodded at him. His hands grasped the steering wheel so tightly his knuckles were white. His lips were a tight white line on his face and his beautifully plucked brows were drawn.

After a few minutes he said, "Nothing is ever normal with you, is it? I love you, but I think I am going to stop asking you questions before you tell me Mil is a vampire and the president is a zombie."

"Well, if there are vampires and zombies I don't know about them, but I didn't know about werewolves until a few days ago."

"Great, your confidence is overwhelming me," Troy said with a scoff. "Speaking of Mil, does she know I am coming?" said he continued with a tight smile. Mil did not like Troy. She couldn't get over him being gay and acting more feminine than I do. And, Troy being Troy loved every second of making her squirm.

"Nope, not a clue," I said with a big smile.

"Fan-freaking-tastic." Troy parked in Mil's driveway. There was a devious sparkle in that man's eyes and I knew I should be worried.

Mil lived in a small two-bedroom, ranch-style brick house. Her closest neighbor was about three acres away. Mil would always say how she could not be close to the earth if people were on top of her. I could see her standing in the doorway and she did not look amused at the sight of Troy.

Mill stood at the great height of five foot even and could not be ninety pounds soaking wet. While Mil may look not a day over ninety, even though she's eighty-seven, she was fighting with the amount of power within her. She looked like a strong wind may set her adrift to the sunset.

"Aye, I see you brought the girly boy with you!" Mil yelled. *Sweet mother of God she did not just say that.* Mil's small frame seemed to fill the doorway in an unnatural way. She had her best Peter Pan stance going on, hands on her hips and her feet spread.

"Aye, Professor McGonagall, she did. And you know you love me, so stop pretending!" Troy bellowed in his best Irish accent. Which, by the way, was pure awful. *Oh sweet hot sauce.* I needed to put these two in a room and let them fight it out battle royale style. But, Troy did have a point; she did look a bit like Harry Potter's professor, but there was no pepper to her hair. It was all stark white. As we got closer to the door, her gray eyes narrowed at Troy.

"What are ya wearin', boy? It looks like women's clothing."

Troy looked down at himself. He had on a black tank top. Not too bad until you got to his bottom half. He had on a pair of tight blue jeans and over that he wore a black sheer skirt. A long one, too. I think he did it just to get a rise out of Mil.

"There's no such thing as women's or men's clothing. It's just who can rock it should wear it. And I," he said while twirling, "rock it."

"Boy, I wouldn't be so sure about that."

"Mil!" I said, pushing past both of them, getting inside the house before a tree mysteriously fell on Troy. "It's good to see you."

"Aye, girl, I did not know you were bringing him," Mil said as she closed the door behind her and Troy.

I opened my mouth to tell her, but was abruptly cut off by Troy's words, "Oh Mil, her car broke down and she needed a ride and when I found her she was busy with—"

"That's fine!" I gave Troy a *"say another word and I'll make you a real woman"* glare and he looked amused.

"Sorry, Mil, I was getting busy. I mean, I got busy." Heat rushed to my face. Could this visit get worse, please? With sugar on top? Troy was trying but failing to stifle a laugh. I shot him a murderous look that only seemed to make him laugh harder.

112

Mil raised one eyebrow at me, but didn't question, thank God. She held out her small arms and her eyes squinted with a smile. I embraced my great aunt. She hugged me so fiercely I feared the tiny woman would break me.

"Mil, what's wrong? Are you okay?" I asked, pulling back and searching her eyes for some kind of emotion. But, like always, there was little to be found in her gray eyes.

"You act like you haven't seen me in a few years when it has only been a few weeks."

"Aye, don't worry yourself. I am fine. But, we have a lot to talk about. So, let's eat," she said, smiling. But, the smile didn't reach her eyes. Something was wrong, I just didn't know what. I'm not sure how much more bad news I could take.

Dinner was a beer-battered pot roast with carrots, potatoes, and onions. Mil would marinade everything in beer if she could. I could have done without the onions, as they are spawn of the devil, but it was what it was.

"Whew, girl, I am glad I brought my big girl panties because Mil it's a flat-out sin for you to cook the way you do!" Troy said with a very satisfied look upon his face.

Laughing, I said, "You gonna be able to drive home? There was an awful lot of beer in that."

"Pfft, don't you worry your pretty self. I got this."

"Ahem, Lainey girl, I need talk to ya about…" she paused, "…private things," she finished with a scowl directed at Troy.

"Oh, you old bat, you mean witchy things?" Troy said while picking his teeth with a toothpick. *Oh my God, he did not just say that! Did he?*

Mil shot me a murderous glance. All I could do was shrug and smile in apology. She threw her wrinkly arms in the air in an act of exasperation.

"Ah girl, can you not keep your mouth shut. And to HIM nonetheless. Sierra, God love her, I could understand, but HIM, ach!" She spat the word *him* as if it were a curse word.

I quickly glanced at Troy and saw him seething in his seat. Before he went all Mount Vesuvius I said, "Mil, I know you love Troy because I love him. I would never keep what I am from him. Please respect that it was my choice to trust him. I love you, Mil, I would never knowingly put us in danger."

Mil and Troy seemed to ease at my words.

"Okay, Lainey girl, well there are something's in regards to Sierra I need to tell you."

"I'm all ears and Troy is, well, he won't say a single word," I said with a bright smile. Troy raised his right hand with three fingers up and with his left he drew a cross over his heart, then mock zipped his lips closed. Clearly I needed to check the sky for flying pigs.

"Okay, girl, I need to tell you the history of our people. I know I have avoided this, but I can no longer."

"Our people were not always known as witches. We can

114

date ourselves back to near 800 BCE. We were called Druids back then. Our abilities were passed down in blood lines back then, but now the lines have gotten so diluted it's rare if there are two or three in the same line. Back then our powers were more than they are today. Just about every Druid's power level would be about seven or eight whereas today it's about a three or four. Also we could change our forms in to that of a beast."

"Beast? What kind of beast?" My heart was racing. She had never in my life been this open about witches before. *I wish had a note pad.*

"Most Druids could shift into wolves. Some bears. And very few hawks. These powers died out long ago and became something else."

"Werewolves," I whispered. My head was spinning and a fog seemed to settle in with every word she spoke.

"Aye, girl, I knew you would find out about them eventually. Werewolves and witches split off from Druids."

"You knew about werewolves and didn't tell me? And how did this split happen?" I was incredulous. *How could she?* I knew there was no masking the anger on my face.

"Lainey, please listen; I had my reasons. Please let me finish." The look on her wrinkled face gave me pause and dampened my anger. I took a deep breath and flipped my hand, signing for her to continue.

"Back when the Druids had their full power, they had to pay a tithe every twenty years to the God Taranis. As the political power in Ireland changed hands, there was an order to stop the tithes from being paid. That is when the split was thought to have happened."

"Mil, what kind of tithe?" I said in my best neutral tone. But, inside I was shivering and I had an idea of what the tithe was. *Please, Mil, don't say what I think you're going to say.*

She drew in a deep breath and spoke as evenly as I have ever heard her, "Girl, they were human sacrifices. Typically young girls."

I couldn't even think, much less speak. The power I had within me wasn't some genetic mishap or anomaly. It was all based in murder. My whole life I thought I lost the genetic lottery, which was probably still true, but I was a product of power-hungry assholes. Holy shit, the Coven had to know this and was willfully hiding it.

"Why is the Coven hiding this?"

"Partly because they did not want the werewolves to become public."

"Why?"

"Girl, let me finish!" Mil scolded.

I crossed my arms over my chest, as if that were going to stop me from blurting out. Hey, a girl can hope.

"The Coven is about power. You know that is part of why I left. Well, they do not want the werewolves public because they do not want political power to be shifted from the Coven to another political structure. The Coven has a plan to take over the governmental system…"

I opened my mouth to explain how asinine that plan was but was stopped by Mil's stare and promptly shut my mouth, causing my teeth to snap.

"Aye, yes it is an awful plan. They are corrupt and power hungry. But, girl, that's not the only reason I left." Mil seemed to be discomforted by whatever this news was, and how it connected to Sierra I have no idea. Mil drew in a pained breath and said, "Do you remember when your ma called me? To tell me about you?"

"Yeah, I was about four when I accidentally electrocuted Frankie."

"Oh sweet baby Jesus you killed someone when you were four?" Troy blurted with a horrified look on his face.

I raised my eyebrow at him as if saying, *really?*

I rolled my eyes and said, "Okay, Frankie was our cat and I will tell you he lived! I have not killed anyone..." then under my breath added, "...yet."

Troy's gazed narrowed at me. "Bitch, I heard that," he said, rolling his eyes back at me.

"Well, after your ma called me, I knew what you were."

What I was? This woman raised me and this was the first time she was ever this forthcoming.

"Mil, as if I haven't asked this question a million times, why am I the only witch who controls lightning? What am I?"

"It is said in the seventh century at the last sacrifice there was a prophecy given through the lifeless body of the tithe.

It was said that the God Taranis spoke directly through her; that with the new times came the new changes. It told of the split of the witches and werewolves from the Druids. And as witches, we cannot be turned into werewolves. But, Taranis foretold there would be one born of him, a child who was born of the storm. And that this child could be turned into a werewolf and with her life's sacrifice, she would rise as a wolf. With her new birth would be the downfall of the witches."

I opened my mouth and abruptly shut it. *There is no damned way.* I mean, there was no way my luck was that damned bad! *I refuse to believe it.* Didn't people smoke all kinds of crazy shit back then? Isn't it possible it was all some hallucination of some guy chasing the dragon?

"Mil, you mean to tell me you moved me around my whole life because you believe in some prophecy rattled off by some mad person? There is no way this thing is true and if it were there's no way it would be me!"

Mil looked at me, practically saying she thought me daft.

"Mil, I love you, but this is insane, you know that, right?" I just couldn't wrap my brain around all of this. "So, you have been forcing me to move every nine months because some prophecy says that some witch will get turned into a werewolf and bring down the Coven?"

Mil's head bobbed up and down in affirmation.

I closed my eyes and pinched the bridge on my nose. I

could feel the headache forming.

"Mil, what does this have to do with Sierra?"

"Don't you see? The werewolves have found out about the prophecy and are killing witches until they find you. Do not try to tell me you have not put yourself into the investigation. I know the weres have been hired to cover this up as quickly as possible. I know you."

She was kidding, right? My whole life was based on the ranting of a group of power-hungry crazy people. How did she know about this?

"Delaney, she means mister yummy pants I saw at your place before we came here," Troy added, ever-so-helpful human that he was.

I gave Troy a look that promised retribution, which did not faze him a bit.

"He was just there to talk about the case! Nothing more!" Sheesh. Way to toss my ass under that bus!

Troy opened his mouth as if to add to my predicament. I pointed my finger at him and a spark flew from it.

"Do not make me electrocute you."

With that his mouth shut with a clack of teeth. He narrowed his eyes at me and said, "Do and you get to pay the bill to my hairstylist."

"Delaney, ask your werewolf when all of these witches died. I know what he will say. On or near the full moon, and I would say their bodies were found near the new moon after they failed to rise."

Speechless. It'd been what, near a week that Sierra died. Wait, Reid said he did not want to get involved because it was too close to the full moon. Could Mil have something? Could she be right? God, the thought of that was so insane it shouldn't even be a thought. Mil and I were going to end up in the loony bin, I swear to God.

"He's not my wolf." That sounded forced even to my ears.

"Laney girl, it's time to move. We need to outrun them and—"

"No," I cut her off in a low and controlled tone. I would not run. I had more power in me than she gave me credit for. I would not be afraid of some prophecy that may never even happen and one that was in no way about me.

"Mil, I will not run. This is all so ridiculous; I can't give it much more thought. I have power, Mil. I can protect myself," I said, standing up. I was more than ready to go.

"Laney, I know you can. Your power level is that of the inner circle. But, your heart will make blind what your head is trying to see. Ask your were. Ask him when they died. And for God's sake do not fall in love with him. I can see something in you changing."

"I do not love him!" I walked over to the door and turned around, both Mil and Troy looking at me with a shared look of incredulity plastered on their faces. I scoffed, which didn't seem to help my case a bit.

"Troy, let's go. Please." I was so done here. I found out a

lot about who I was, and most of it was a lie. If she kept talking, I may find out I was born a lobster.

"Laney girl, please think about leaving. I beg you."

"I love you, Mil. I'll see you soon," I said as I walked out the front door. I couldn't hug her and I couldn't even stand to look at her much longer. I had to just leave all of this insanity behind me.

THE WHOLE WAY HOME I VACILLATED ON WHETHER OR not I should call Reid and ask him. If I called him, would that mean I believed Mil? If I didn't, would I sit and question everything and every one of his motivations?

I plopped on my couch and scents of Reid wafted up to greet me. I closed my eyes and breathed him in. Flashes of us entered my mind. His hands on me, his lips on me, oh sweet hot sauce. My body felt flushed and heat rushed to my core and my belly tightened. What almost happened on this couch? *Oh holy hell.* I picked up the phone and dialed.

"Hey, Delaney." Reid's smooth liquid voice seemed to pour from the phone and lick lightly at my earlobe. "Delaney, are you there? Is everything okay?" Belatedly, I realized I had not said a damned word.

"Oh yes, sorry. Hi, Reid. I just got back from Mil's house and she told me all kinds of things, like basically my life was..." I trailed off, mainly because I realized I was rambling. Delaney, get this this together!

"Sorry, I was rambling, I have a silly question."

"Okay, shoot."

"So the ten girls who were killed. Was there a specific time of the month they were killed? Something that linked them?"

Silence. The silence seemed to go on forever. *Please, Reid, say no. Just say no*.

Finally, after a small eternity, Reid said, "Delaney, what are you asking?"

Oh God, no please. "Reid, tell me. You know what I am asking."

I heard Reid take a deep breath and let it out. "Yes, they were all killed on or near the full moon."

It was a slap in the face. How could he not have told me this?

"Delaney, please listen to me. It is impossible for a were to turn a witch. I told you this. I do not know what it seems this guy is trying, but he is."

"You didn't think it was a good idea to tell me? Reid, I am a witch, did you not think this was good information for me to have? Or is it simply you don't trust me?" I spat the words as if they were poison on my tongue.

"Delaney, please, it is impossible to turn a witch. I didn't think it mattered. I thought you would over react."

Did he really go there? The pure and simple fact was he didn't trust me. Sure, he'd only known me a few days at most, but someone seemed to think the prophecy could be true. If he didn't trust me with that information, then maybe I should keep my own recently learned facts to myself. For now, at least. If there was some dimwit out there killing witches to try to change them to a werewolf, then telling a werewolf might be a bad idea.

"Look, Reid, I need time. My world has been turned upside down and I am not sure there is a place for you in it. I still want to get this asshole and I will be there for that. But, please give me some space." God, why did the words seem to burn my heart as I said them?

One heartbeat, two, three ... Silence.

"Reid?"

"Yeah, Delaney, I'll give you space. Is there anything else?" he said in a clipped and detached tone.

Why did his tone hurt? Didn't I want space to decide if I could trust him? Wasn't this the path I choose to walk down?

"N-no. I guess I'll talk to you later." Wait, wasn't I supposed to be the one with hurt feelings? Wasn't I supposed to be the mad one? Then why did my heart feel like it was being ripped out of my chest?

"Okay b..." I started, then realized he hung up already.

Well, Delaney, time to go lay in that bed you made.

REID JAMISON

NINE

S HADES OF BETH ALL OVER AGAIN. I HELD THE PHONE in my hand, desperately trying not to take my frustration out on the damned device. Space. She needed space. That's all I have been wanting to give her this whole time was space. Space to stop my body from reacting to her. Space to stop myself from getting attached to her. All the space did was make me want her more. I knew it was this damned mating call, but I did not want it, or at least that's what I kept telling myself. I swore many years ago that I would not get involved with any woman, not after Beth.

My grip tightened on the phone, shattering the screen. *Shit. Fantastic.* Now on top of all of these issues my phone's screen was busted. Why? Why did this girl have this kind of effect on me? I threw the phone on the bed before I sat on the edge, causing the bed to dip to one side. I closed my eyes and let the memory of Beth consume me.

16 October 1959

Beth would kill me if I was late for dinner again. I glanced down at my wrist watch. 5:36 P.M. Damn, I was already late. I looked at the huge pile of folders and glanced at my watch again, resigned myself to the fact that I would be missing dinner. A Friday night and here I was working on depositions for my slave driver of a boss. I should be thankful for this job, as it provided for Beth and what would someday be a family, I hoped. The thought of the children we have yet to conceive thrilled me. Beth was twenty-three and we had been married for three years, and been trying ever since to have children. It would happen someday soon. The thought made me smile. I glanced down at my watch again; it read 9:02 P.M. Damnit. I stood up from my desk and gathered my things, placing them in my briefcase. I was leaving, paperwork done or not. I wanted to see Beth.

We lived in a small city just outside of Chicago, only a few miles from my office, so to save money I walked to work. We picked this area because we thought raising a family here would be just what we wanted. Plus, I was lucky to find work with the only lawyer in town right away.

The night was fairly brisk and I pulled my overcoat snugly around my neck, as I had forgotten my scarf back at the office. I was about a quarter mile into my two-mile trek when I got the distinct feeling I was being followed. For the first ten minutes, I chalked it up to it being so late and the fog rolling in. But, when the feeling did not abate, I began to survey my surroundings. There was a wide patch of trees between my office and my house, and the trees were strangely still in the October night.

About then I began to hear noises. I heard the sound of brush being moved and disturbed. Then what sounded like multiple soft footfalls on the dried leaves. I began hearing a low growl. I froze. I saw its eyes first. I use the term IT because IT was too big to be some kind of animal I knew of. Out of the dense tree line stood a massive dog or wolf. The animal slowly paced back and forth a few feet at a time. I swallowed and walked forward on my path. The beast continued to pace from a few hundred feet away. Oh God, what if I led this thing home to Beth? There was no way on Earth I was going to let that happen.

"What do you want, beast?" I called to it. At the sound of my voice the animal's ears pricked and he paused in his rhythmic pacing. Within the blink of an eye, the creature was less than fifty feet away. At this distance I didn't know how I could have ever mistaken him for a mutt, for this creature was not merely a dog. He looked like a demon wolf with glowing yellow eyes.

Within another blink, the creature was a scant three feet from me. It began pacing tight circles around me. I had a sinking feeling in my stomach, but I would fight this beast if he attacked. I would fight for Beth. The creature was impossibly fast; I knew that when it lunged at my throat and I had little time to fend it off. I pounded and fought like a wild beast myself.

I never felt the pain; only the thought of run, get away, registered. I only felt his teeth slide farther into my neck. With yet another impossibly fast jerk the animal was done. I tried to get up, but my limbs felt heavy and my head began to feel foggy.

When did I put cotton in my ears? I licked my too-dry lips and tasted something like iron, was that blood? My vision began to get spotty. Finally, after what seemed like an eternity, I was able to lift my mangled left hand to my throat, only to find most of it missing. I could feel myself slipping into the darkness. I fought it. But, in the end, it was all for naught. I am so sorry, Beth. I let go and slipped into the blackness.

14 January 1960

Three months of running. Fleeing, really. Fleeing from what I have turned into. I spent three months desperately trying to control and cage this beast inside me. The animal who did this to me I had not seen since I rose, two weeks after my apparent death. After the beast ripped my throat out, it dragged me to a nearby alcove in a heavily wooded area, where I lay bleeding out. When I woke, I knew I shouldn't be alive. No man went through what I had, just to wake up two weeks later as if it were some nap.

My eyes flew open and I began to gasp for much-needed air. I was immediately bombarded with scents. I could smell dried blood, dead leaves, wet earth, and sweat. It wasn't until that last smell that I knew whatever had done this to me was still there.

"I know you're here," I managed to rasp. My eyes were shut tight, as the colors and light were too much for my reeling brain to handle. What the hell had happened?

"Ah yes, new one, I am here, I am glad to see you turned successfully," a man said with a light Eastern European accent.

I cracked my eyes to see this creature. I was blinded with light for a solid thirty seconds before my eyes got used to the vivid colors that surrounded me. The greens were brighter and the blacks did not look as dark. My eyes shifted left to right before falling upon a tall lanky man of forty or so. He wore a hairstyle that was not common for men, and what looked to be shoulderlength black hair that was bound back. His eyes were such a deep brown they appeared to be black. His face was made up of narrow angles and sharp lines leading to a long and somewhat pointed chin. Either he had not shaved in the last few days or he took his 5 o'clock shadow seriously. That reminded me and I reached up toward my neck and felt only my slightly stubbled skin as if I had shaved that morning. My eyes flew to this man, who I knew in my soul had done this to me.

Finding my voice, I asked, "What did you do to me?"

The man's dark eyebrow raised and a smile slowly spread across his face. The gesture unnerved me, but I would not show fear, for if I did I had a feeling this man would exploit it.

"I gave you gift. You will hunt and you will live. And more."

"You call this a gift?" I scoffed. Was he insane? I looked at his face. Well, insane may be correct.

"I call it a gift because it is." He went on to explain what exactly I was and what that meant. A monster. He had turned me into a monster. I felt the rage bubble up and begin to spill over. My fists clenched and unclenched. I wanted to kill him. I could kill him. I had visions of me charging him and ripping his head clean off his body. I stood up and walked past him. I needed to

get home to Beth.

"Where are you going?"

"Home to my wife. If you come near me again I will kill you," I said in a low, measured tone. I needed him to understand that if I indeed did see him, I would kill him.

I felt a strong hand on my arm. I froze, trying to rein in my temper. I was always so even keeled; this new rage was going to take some getting used to.

"You need to control your wolf before you go to her. Or you could kill her."

It was the words "you could kill her" that had me turning around.

"I would never…"

"You would! If you got mad enough, you would."

That was all it took for me to erupt. I had his neck in my hand and his body pushed up against a tree before I could register what it was I was doing.

A strained smile played on his face as he rasped, "All it takes is one time. Now I will tell you what you need to do."

I was ready after three months of fighting for control, three months of hunting to satisfy the beast. I stood on my front doorstep resting my forehead on the door. I could hear Beth moving around in the house. I could smell that she was baking cookies, but moreover I could smell Beth. She smelled of lavender and lemons.

Finally, I knocked. I heard her soft footfalls on the entry floor. She opened the door and I almost leapt at her with the need to touch her. Her sparkling blue eyes went wide with shock and she began to hyperventilate.

"Beth! I know it is a shock, but please let me in and I swear I can explain." I needed her to understand what I was and how this did not have to change anything.

She looked as though she might pass out. I reached out to her and she cowered back. She was afraid of me.

"Please," I begged.

"F-f-fine." It seemed to be the only word she was able to effectively communicate.

I walked in the home that Beth and I built and sat on the worn leather couch. Beth sat across from me in an outdated arm chair. I hated that damned chair because it smelled like smoke, but Beth loved the flower print so I couldn't say no to her when she begged me to get it.

Her blonde curls bobbed slightly as she spoke, "Where the hell have you been? I had the police looking for you and there you just show up three months later?"

Part of the time I spent away was planning on what I was going to say to her. Do I lie or tell the truth? In the end I would tell her the truth, all of it. But for now I lied. I explained how I had been hit by a car and the driver took me over to the next town over to the big hospital in Chicago.

I think that she wanted to believe the lies because she just got up kissed me on the cheek and walked into the kitchen and life went on that way for months. In that time our life went back to normal. I got my job back and we resumed trying for a baby.

I knew trying was useless because it would never happen now that I was a monster. Every month it didn't happen, her smile seemed to falter and fall even more than before. After six months of watching her vibrant light darken to a mere flicker, I knew I would have to tell her soon. Then maybe she would want to change too.

One day, after work, I sat down to wait for her to return from her trip to from the store. I would tell her today. Finally, after what seemed to be an eternity, she walked in the back door. I got up and walked over to her. We did what we had been doing for several months now: walking around each other in silence. It was maddening.

"Beth, we need to talk."

She looked at me with a resigned look on her face. It seemed like she knew I was upset with our current relationship, but I know she could never guess why. I took in a deep breath and told her the truth. All of it.

She sat there unmoving for a long time.

"Beth?"

"If you wanted to leave because I could not have children, you should have just never come back," she said softly.

The mention of children spiked a knife through my heart.

"Beth, I'm not lying. I could show you."

She stood up abruptly and smoothed her skirt down.

"Fine. Then show me."

I slowly got up and went into the kitchen. I began to strip my clothes off.

"Please just give me a few minutes alone."

"Okay!" she hollered back then in a low tone said, "He's nuts. I am going to have to get him electric shock therapy or something."

Thank goodness it was a full moon tonight and the change only took a few minutes. I shook out my body and made my way in to the den. Her back was to me and I sat down just inside the entrance of the doorway. She didn't turn around so I sneezed. She turned around made eye contact with the wolf. Again her eyes went wide and she fainted.

I placed a cool rag on her forehead and began to whisper to her. I was in a bit of pain from two quick transitions, but it was for Beth.

"Beth, honey. My love, please wake up," I crooned.

She began to wake, but slowly.

"I had an awful dream," she murmured.

"Shhh, I know, love."

Her eyes popped open and focused on me. She bolted up in a seated position and scrambled to get away from me.

"Y-y-you're a monster!" Her words broke my heart entirely.

"No, do I look different? Am I different? Beth, I am still your Reid," I pleaded with her. I had lost my humanity; I would not lose her too. "Please give me a chance. I am begging you. This is why we could not have children these past few months. But, I promise you we can adopt a hundred children." I got up and left the room to give her space. About an hour later she sat across from me and spoke.

"Yes, I will try." It took everything within me not to pounce on her and devour her mouth and take her where she sat.

How stupid I was to think she would really try. Three days later I came home from work to find her lifeless body hanging from our bedroom doorway. She didn't leave a note. But her lifeless body was note enough. The message was clear. I would rather die than love a monster.

The hotel phone rang, scrambling the memories. I moved to answer it.

"What?" I spat at the phone.

"Hey, Captain Polite, what's the plan? Heard from Delaney?" Mitch's tinny voice rang from the phone.

"Meet me at the car. We are going to find Cowboy Bill," I said as I hung up the phone.

Delaney may need space, but I had a job to do and it was less than four weeks until the next full moon. I refused to let another person die because some werewolf was having a delusion of changing a witch. I would not let my attraction to her hinder me from finding this asshole. Cowboy Bill was literally the only lead we had, and I had to find him.

"Hey, Delaney," I said into the phone. I would not crack this one.

"Oh, um, hi, Reid. What's up?" Delaney's cold tone seemed to spark from the phone and sputter to the floor.

"Hey, thought I would let you know we are going to look for Cowboy Bill. I thought I would see if you wanted to come along."

There was a prolonged pause and I knew what she would say. The same thing she had been saying for the past three weeks.

"Yeah, I'm sorry, Reid. I, um, have to work. Ronald said he needed me at the store today. Sorry." The lie in her voice was palpable.

"Yeah, okay." It was hard to hide the disappointment in my voice.

"Okay b—"

I hung up the phone. I had no interest in being blown off again. I didn't think she knew I knew she was lying.

Delaney had no idea about two weeks ago I went to see Ronald at the record store and he said she never came in after she somehow "torched the place." The guy looked like a gremlin, so I tuned out everything else he said and moved on.

Nearly three weeks she had been dodging my calls. Well, today was the day I would go get her. I honestly couldn't care less that she was pissed, but this wasn't about her. We had looked daily for this guy and in the end we did not know Savannah and needed her to help direct us. The homeless community wandered, but I knew Delaney would know where to go.

I pounded on her door. I would not let her sulk and

avoid me because I fucked something up. I heard a brief rustling the and soft, "Shit" from behind the poorly painted door. I inhaled, hoping to catch her scent through the door. There it was. Ozone and gardenias. I would never have thought that scent would plague my dreams, but it did. The woman had burrowed under my skin. I needed her scent like I needed air.

"Delaney, open the damned door. I can hear you."

No answer. She wanted to play hardball, did she? Game on, my little firecracker. If she thought her friend, what was his name, ah, Troy, could make a scene, she had no idea what I could do.

"Delaney, I can smell you," I nudged. I wanted to see how far she would let me take this.

Silence. I smiled.

In a much louder voice I said, "Remember what happened the last time I said that? I kissed you, then you wrapped your legs around me and…"

The door flew open. I almost laughed. *So predictable.*

"Reid! God, what are you doing here?" she said, a little wild-eyed.

I hadn't seen her in what, three weeks, and now her storm-cloud eyes almost had me babbling. My eyes traveled down her small turned-up nose to her full bow-shaped lips and I was remembering how those soft lips tasted. My eyes continued their journey down her body. She had on a ratty shirt with fifty or so small holes in it. She clearly did not have a bra on, as I could see the outline of her pink-tipped breasts. I flicked my eyes lower and stopped in shock.

"Look, Reid, why are you here?" She put her hands on her hips.

I met her gaze. She had no pants on. When she put her hands on her hips, her shirt rose to show a beautiful pink thigh and I almost let loose a growl. My pants were beginning to fit a little snug. *Damn this female for having such an effect on me.*

"Can we take this inside?" I barely managed to say it without snarling.

"No, we most certainly cannot! You're not answering any of my questions."

Delaney Hagen was put on this Earth to infuriate me. That had to be her sole mission in life. In the most even tone I could manage I said, "Delaney, you have no pants on. So, I would think you would want to take this inside."

Her eyes went wide and she looked down at her bare legs. When she met my eyes again her beautiful round face was a beautiful shade of pink.

"Oh my God," she said, turning and running inside the apartment. When she turned and ran away the wind kicked up the back of her shirt and I got a brief glance at her ass. Were those kittens?

"Stay at the door! Do not sit down. Do not make yourself at home."

"So much for southern hospitality," I countered.

Three minutes later Delaney came out of her bedroom. Gone was the ratty T-shirt. It was replaced by a black-ribbed tank top that read, "Holy hot sauce, Batman!" and much to my disappointment she seemed to have put a bra on. And she had on little khaki shorts.

She was putting her hair up in some kind of messy thing on the top of her head when she said, "Sorry. Now, why are you here?"

"It's time to stop sulking. We need your help to find Bill."

"I am not sulking!" she said in a tone much like a petulant child would have used. She seemed to realize her tone and said, "Look I just don't have time. I have to work."

"I saw Ronald two weeks ago. He said you haven't been back since you torched the place, whatever that means."

"Oh God, you blow up one register and three security cameras and he says I'm burning the joint down," she scoffed.

"You're avoiding me."

She looked at the floor. She kicked the rug with her bare toe.

"Delaney, I should have told you. But, I didn't think it mattered as it's impossible."

Without looking up she whispered, "What if it's not impossible?"

I closed the distance between us and placed a finger under her chin to draw her eyes to mine.

"Look, it is impossible. I am not making this up. I need

137

your help. Sierra needs your help."

"That was dirty. And you know it. I will help but…" she paused, seeming to look for the right words. "But US can't happen again, Reid."

I knew that. I would have said the same thing had she not said it first. But, then why did those words hurt? Why did it feel like Beth all over again?

"I know. Just get your shoes," I said and walked out of the apartment to go wait for her in the Jeep.

"Okay, so we have spent the last few weeks running around in circles trying to find Cowboy Bill. There are about seven days left until the next full moon. We have scoured the homeless camp. The only thing we have found is that Cowboy Bill is still in town, but is laying low. We do not know where to go from here and thought you could help."

The whole time I was speaking, she was looking out the window. She was deliberately avoiding my gaze. She was insufferable! The better question though was why did I want to see her storm-cloud eye dance when she looked at me?

A few minutes later she spoke softly, "Have you tried bringing him dinner?"

I raised my eyebrow at her. Bring him dinner? Was she serious?

"Um no, I did not realize I should be dating him."

Delaney looked at me as if I had sixteen heads. "If I rolled my eyes any more my eyeballs would get stuck in my skull. Reid, trust me. We need to go get him dinner."

"Aye aye, Captain."

About twenty minutes later we were back in the Jeep with a heaping mound of rice and teriyaki chicken and about a gallon of an orange liquid called shrimp sauce. When I asked why we needed it since we did not get shrimp, Delaney informed me it was a *"moral imperative."* I picked up the phone to call Mitch and let him know the plan.

"Saldana."

"Mitch, hey, we are going to the bridge."

"About damn time. Where the hell have you been? I've been waiting forever over here."

I paused to look at Delaney and said, "Apparently, we are dating Cowboy Bill and had to pick him up dinner."

There was a long pause. I knew Mitch was thinking I was insane.

"Just meet us there."

"Shall I bring the wine?" Mitch said in a petulant tone.

I hung up.

It took about another twenty minutes for Mitch to pull up next to us. Delaney rolled down her window and gave Mitch a dazzling smile.

"Hey, Mitch! Good to see you."

It took everything in me not to jump out the car and throttle Mitch.

"Hey, beautiful! Missed seeing you," Mitch said. His arms were both above him resting on the doorframe, allowing him to hang his head in the window. His face was entirely too close to Delaney. I took a deep breath and tried to wrangle the beast down. These reactions were insane.

"Delaney, you seem to have a plan here. Would you mind enlightening us?" I said in a half growl. Mitch seemed to take a cue from my tone and met my gaze. His intense stare asked if this would be an issue working with her. I just shook my head.

"I do. Mitch do you have a twenty on you?"

Mitch raised his eyebrows in question.

"Oh come on. As I am sure you both know I got fired so to make this work I need a little cash." She put her palm out and waved her fingers back and forth as if to say, *come on, you moron, give me what I want.*

Mitch dug in his pocket and slapped a twenty in her hand.

"Okay, now what?" Mitch questioned.

"You two stay here and I will bring him back here."

Both Mitch and I looked from each other back to her. Was she kidding? There was no way in hell I was letting her go in there by herself.

"Yeah that's not going to happen, Delaney," I said what Mitch and I were both thinking.

She looked over at me and narrowed her eyes at me and said in a flat tone, "I can take care of myself."

I swear I saw lightning spark behind her eyes.

Without taking my eyes off hers I said to Mitch, "Let her out, let's see if she can best the big bad wolves." Before she moved to get out, I put my hand on hers. A tingle went through me at the point of contact.

"Be careful." Her face seemed to pinken slightly.

"I will." She got out of the car, but not before I caught her scent on the wind. I smiled at her back. I knew what scent that was and it only roused the wolf.

"So we aren't really going to let her go in there by herself, are we?" Mitch said in an amused tone.

Laughing, I said, "Fuck no."

"Yeah, didn't think so."

It only took us three minutes to find Delaney walking through the camp. She passed by about every person as if she knew just who she was looking for. She seemed to spot someone, for her stride had purpose. She stood in front of a child who could not have been more than about ten. Mitch and I were several yards away trying to be in earshot yet not be seen. For a werewolf that was fairly easy, as we have excellent hearing.

"Hi, I'm Delaney! What's your name?" Delaney said in a bright tone. She bent down slightly to be eye to eye with the little boy. The position emphasized her shapely ass and I tried not to groan at the sight of her. I heard Mitch next to me and it seemed he had not missed the provocative position in the slightest.

"I'm Ben. You don't belong here," the little boy said with affirmation.

"I know, Ben. But, I need your help finding someone."

"I-I don't know, I'm not supposta help, um…" The little boy's voice trailed off. Looked like she was running into the same issues Mitch and I faced. These people had a tight-knit community and outsiders were not welcome.

"Oh okay, Ben, I guess I will have to find someone else to give this to." She waved around the twenty-dollar bill.

The little boy Ben seemed to light up and all but yelled, "Wait! No, I can help!"

Delaney gave the boy a knowing smile and said, "Wow, really? Well, I need you to go get Cowboy Bill for me. Tell him I brought him dinner."

The little boy frowned at Delaney and said, "That's it?"

"Yup, that's it!"

"Okay, stay here! I'll be back!" the boy said, running off.

I looked over at Mitch and he had the same look of incredulity I was sure was on my face. Delaney had done more with twenty damned dollars and a box of food than we had in three fucking weeks. *Is this reality?*

Suddenly Delaney seemed to look right at me as if she knew I was there. Mitch leaned over and whispered in my ear, "Do you think she sees us?"

I softly scoffed, "No way."

Then she raised her right hand in our general direction and preceded to tell us we were number one. Mitch guffawed.

"Did she just flick us off?"

"Yeah, she did," I laughed back. "I guess we should go

back to the car, seems as though she's got this taken care of."

"Yeah, man, what I wouldn't mind doing to her. She's feisty. I like that," Mitch said nonchalantly.

I stopped dead in my tracks. I was actively trying not to bash his face in. Mitch seemed to notice something was wrong and turned to me.

"Look, Reid, I know there's some tension with the two of you, but we talked about how you were not interested in claiming her. She is free for me to pursue if we both want it," Mitch stated matter-of-factly.

And he was right. I mean, what could I say to that? I would not claim her despite this mating call. Then why was I acting like such a tool? I did want Delaney, but enough to claim her? She was such a wild card. She was stunning and her body was ... Well, it could make a monk rethink his vow of celibacy.

It took about twenty minutes for Delaney to round the corner of the camp and walk to the Jeep. Behind her trailed who I thought was Ben, but upon closer inspection the person tailing Delaney stood no taller than four feet, had a rather round belly, and a beard ZZ Top would be envious of. The short man also wore a worn cowboy hat atop his head.

I pushed away from the car to get a better look at this guy. Before I could make my way to the small man I heard a thick Texas drawl say, "Where muh tea? Girl here said there would be sweet tea."

I raised an eyebrow at the man. "You must be Cowboy

Bill."

The short man looked me over and had to squint to do so, as the light was fading.

"I am, and you have got to be the biggest son-a-bitch I ever did see."

"Bill! Don't be rude!" Delaney scolded.

"Sorry, ma'am," Bill said, seeming to be somewhat embarrassed. And with that, my assessment of the man went up appreciably.

"Bill, my name is Reid Jamison and this is my partner, Mitch Saldana. We have been looking for you for some time and we have a few questions to ask you, if you don't mind."

"I know you been lookin' for me. I been avoidin' you," he said as he awkwardly held on to the box of food.

"Bill, how about you hop up on this truck and while you eat we will ask you a few questions. Then we will leave you alone," Mitch suggested.

Cowboy Bill eyed Mitch, then me. He sighed and walked over to the black Ford. The small man ambled up onto the bed of the truck with more grace than I would have given him credit for. That's what I got for judging that book based on the cover.

"Bill, you called 911 to report someone dragging a body. Can you tell us what you saw?" Mitch asked.

"Well," Cowboy Bill said around a mouth full of food, "it was hard to see with the brush and all. Oh and I didn't have my glasses." He shoved another forkful of rice in his mouth and kept speaking. Clearly he was not taught not to talk with his mouth full. "So, I went to take a piss and as I was about to wrap things up I hear someone grunting. So I thought it was someone getting down, if you know what I mean. But, then I see this naked guy with blood on him dragging something. I just stood there trying to see, but I got afraid. He had dark hair kinda like yours." He pointed to Mitch. "But, shorter. And then the weirdest thing happens. The guy puts a cell phone to his ear and in a really gruff voice says, 'I got another one. Meet me at the street then I want to meet back in Atlanta.' That's when I ran off and heard him running behind me, but I got to the camp before him. I ran to Athena. She got a phone so I called the cops."

I looked at Mitch and his eyes went incandescent with rage.

"Mitch? Could this be one of yours?" I questioned.

It took him a few seconds to answer as he was clearly fighting his wolf for control.

"I don't know. I didn't think it was. But, if it is I will fucking kill them. Are you sure that's what you heard?" Mitch clearly pronounced each syllable of each word.

Cowboy Bill stopped mid-shovel and glared at Mitch. "Son, I couldn't make out the features on his face, but I know what I heard for sure. His voice sounded like he gargled with a box of rocks and he said just what I told you."

Mitch's hands were clenched into tight fists. He seemed distressed to the max at this news. The thought of having someone in your pack doing this is like a brother or sister doing it. It was incomprehensible. And him being the Alpha of Atlanta made it all the worse. That was part of the reason I was a lone wolf. But, I also didn't have the protection of a pack.

Mitch was seething by the time he reached into his pocket and got his cell phone out. He pounded the numbers in so hard I thought I saw the screen crack.

"Mark, get the pack together for a meeting in seven hours. I have a few things to do here then it will take me about four hours to get there. And, Mark, when I say get the pack, I mean get the whole fucking pack. No fucking excuses. All of them."

There was a pause and Mitch all but growled into the phone, "I don't care how late it is! You get every last goddamned member there or you better pray for mercy to whatever god you worship." And with that his phone shattered. "Shit."

"Bill, that's all we need. Delaney, please give him his tea so he can go. Also, Bill, thank you for your help," I said, never taking my eyes off Mitch. I didn't think I had ever seen my old friend this angry before.

The short man got off the truck and walked over to Delaney and took the tea from her, saying, "You gunna be alright, honey?"

"Oh yeah, their bark is way worse than their bite," she said, eyeing me and Mitch.

Bill tipped his hat to us and left.

"If it was one of mine, Reid, I'll find them. There will be a travel ban put on my pack," Mitch said, not meeting my eyes. Never had this alpha not met my eyes.

Delaney walked over to Mitch and put her hand on his shoulder. In a low, controlled tone said, "Are you okay?"

Mitch looked into her eyes then looked at me, and in that moment I knew his wolf was too close to the surface.

Calmly I walked over to Delaney and snaked an arm around her waist and whispered in her ear, "Go back to the car and get in. No sudden movements." For once Delaney did not question. She seemed to understand the situation. She stood there frozen, then shuddered and stepped aside.

"You need to let me go, if you want me to walk to the car," she whispered back to me.

Reluctantly, I let her go. Before I did, I felt her body shudder against mine. But her words, you need to let me go, hung in the air between us. And at that moment I realized that no, no I would not let her go.

Ten minutes later, Mitch walked to the truck and he said, "I have to go to Atlanta. And if I find him I swear, Reid."

There was no need to finish the statement. He would kill him in a way to cause considerable pain. I smiled at the thought and walked to the car.

DELANEY HAGEN
TEN

Traitorous body! Seriously! My body reacted to Reid in a way that was so not normal! I touched Mitch and I had a reaction of ice compared to the pure unadulterated heat my body experienced with Reid. Thank God the ride to my apartment had not taken that long. Cooped up in a small space with Reid Jamison, well, I could not be held liable if I jumped on him kissed him and raked my fingers ... ugh now I couldn't get my mind off him. First, my body now my mind, what's next? I didn't want to even think about that. Thank God for Troy being at my apartment when I got there.

"Delaney!" Reid called just after I got out of the car. I flinched at the sound of his voice. I couldn't help it. The man had a direct path to my nerves.

I turned around and put my best *"What the hell do you want"* face on.

"Yes?" I said, only managing to keep a little bit of the annoyance out of my voice.

"Listen, you can hate me all you want, but I know you feel what I do." Right as I was going to give my wittiest comeback - I have no idea what it would have been, but assume funny and illuminating - he raised his hand to silence me. Yeah, like that would work. But he kept on talking as though he had control of every facet of the conversation.

"Listen, right now I want you to be careful. There is only a week before the next full moon and I have a feeling this guy isn't done with this yet, and I don't feel as though he has moved yet either."

I rested my forearms on the open window ledge of the Jeep so I could be even with Reid. That was a bad idea. Hot caramel eyes seemed to trap me every time.

"Reid," the name came out a bit more breathless than I had intended. I swallowed. "Listen, I'll be fine. Troy and I are going for a run then I am staying with him tonight. Plus, you have no proof this ass is still here and you would have no idea that he would come after me." I thought about telling him what Mil had told me a few weeks ago, but it sounded crazy to my ears, and besides, I wasn't too sure I could trust Reid.

"I know, Delaney. Please just stay with Troy. And be careful."

"You betcha." I stood up and turned to walk away, but Reid's lightning-fast hand secured around my wrist. I peered down at the shackle circling my wrist then at the man it was attached to. His eyes were now flecked with green.

My heart began to pick up the pace. Reid lifted my hand to his soft warm lips and brushed two feather-light kisses against my knuckles. And just like that warmth seemed to spread throughout my body and settle between my thighs. His lips curved up into a slight smile. Damn him, because he knew what he did to me and he knew I was trying to be mad at him. I narrowed my eyes at him and snatched my hand from his. He shot me a wicked smile and pulled out of the lot.

"What the hell was that about?" Troy's voice rang through the nighttime parking lot.

"You know what, Troy? I think he's hunting me. And I don't mean physically," I said absently.

"Oh, honey, he's most definitely hunting you, and absolutely doing it physically."

AS A RULE I AM NOT THE BIGGEST FAN OF CARS. TROY behind the wheel tended to make me slightly nervous. Thank God the drive from my house to his was only fifteen minutes or so. Troy liked to think the speed limits were just a suggested speed. Sometimes driving with him was like playing an intense game of Frogger. I spent most of the time praying and holding onto the "oh shit" handle as if that would really save me. It sure didn't seem to help my parents when I caused their deaths.

I closed my eyes to get my mind off of Reid and Troy. I thought of my parents and one of the few full-color memories I had of them. The day of the crash.

22 January 1993

I remember wearing a shirt that was bright green with little white flowers on it. My mom wanted me to wear a sweater, but I didn't want to. I didn't like sitting with my back against the car seat and feeling all of the pesky wrinkles. I looked up into my mom's face and remembered how beautiful she was. I hoped so much that when I grew up I would look just like her. She had a full face and a small upturned nose. She had stormy gray eyes, just like mine. But, she was blonde where my hair was mainly brown with glints of red.

"Come on, Delaney, it's time to go see Mil!" my mom's cheery voice chimed though the house.

I loved going to see Mil! I got to use my power with Mil. Mom and Dad did not like for me to use my power in the house. But, sometimes I couldn't help it. It was hard for me to control; this was all so new. It mainly happened when I got upset, excited, or scared.

"Are you calm? You cannot get into the car unless you're calm," my dad's smooth voice sang. He reached up to his brownish-red mop of hair and brushed it out of his eyes.

I smiled and bounced from one foot to the next. "Yes, I'm calm. See!" I said, standing very still.

Dad had a wide, full smile and I loved when he smiled; it made everything light up.

"Okay, pumpkin, let's go."

Mil lived far away from us. It took at least two hours to get there. When my parents would take me to see Mil they did it during naptime so I would sleep in the car, and this was no exception. I remember telling my dad he needed to get his haircut and if he didn't I was not going to share my scrunchies with him. His laughter filled the car and it washed over me like a warm blanket. His laugh always made me feel tingly and warm. I faded off to sleep.

It was always the same dream. It was me standing in a field, alone. I would be standing in a circle surrounded by large stones. I would call for my mommy and daddy, but hear nothing but my own voice echoed back at me. Sometimes I would sit down and wait for whatever it was to happen. Every time I would try to leave the stone circle I would just walk right back into the circle from another direction.

Then I heard it. The snarling and growling. My heart would race and at the time I thought it might beat out of my tiny chest. Only when the monster set foot into the circle would I be allowed to run. I had this dream so many times I knew when I would be allowed to flee. This time the monster was a man with long black hair tied back in a ponytail at the base of his neck. This was the first time the monster was a man. I thought maybe he was here to save me. I took a small step toward him to see if he would make the dreams stop. His smile was all teeth and it made me pause.

152

He licked his lips and in a strange accent said, "Run, little one."

That's just what I did. I ran. My little legs were no match for the monster. I tried everything until I could no longer control my power and let go of the last thread of control.

I woke up to screaming. Tears were streaming down my face. I couldn't remember where I was. I was in the car. Going to see Mil. I looked for my parents, but my vision took time to clear.

"Mom? Dad?" I rasped. There was no reply as the state of the car came into focus.

There was glass in my lap and blood in my hands. That's when I smelled the gas and smoke. I started screaming. I could make out my mom's slumped form in the front passenger's seat and my dad's form in the driver's seat, but neither of them were moving. Someone wrenched open the door.

"Shit, are you okay, honey?" a rough, low male voice said.

I looked at him, but couldn't make out the features on his face. His large hands tugged on my child safety restraints and after a few seconds of tugging and swearing he pulled me out of the car.

"Mommy, Daddy!" I screamed the whole time.

The man ran away from the car with me in his arms. He set me down on the ground, where I was able to see what happened. The front of the car was a crumpled mess. It seemed to be completely wrapped around a tree. There was smoke coming from the engine and underside of the car. All of the damage seemed to be focused on the front, yet the whole back window was blown out and the top of the trunk was black and the paint had bubbled up from extreme heat. It fanned out from a central point. The point was where I was strapped in.

"Stay here, honey. I'll go get your parents," the large man said. He wore a white T-shirt and blue jean overalls. In my child's mind, this man was a farmer. I had a brief thought of, But you're a farmer, not a fireman. *He took one step toward the car and that's when it erupted in flames.*

I remember the heat. It was so intense. The heat seemed to pull out every bit of moisture from my little body. My mouth was too dry and my eyelids felt as if they grated down like sandpaper every time I blinked. The man picked me up and started to walk toward the street. I was screaming for him to take me back to wait for my mommy and daddy. He didn't understand; they would be upset if I weren't there when the fire stopped. I kicked and screamed, but the man's hold on me was like iron. I screamed until I had no more voice and when I had no voice I cried, even though the fire took my tears from me. I passed out. And for the first time in what seemed like my whole life, all five years of it, I didn't dream. How could I? My nightmares were real and I was the monster.

Later, I would find out that there was a catastrophic failure of everything with an electrical charge. While that was not enough to cause the car to crash, it was enough to distract my father and cause him to go off the road and hit the tree. But, how the fire started was a mystery.

"Earth to Delaney!" Troy's voice was a bucket of cold

water on my thoughts. His voice acted like a lifesaver pulling me to the rescue boat.

"Yeah, sorry. Just thinking," I tried to cover. The thought of my parents came from nowhere.

"Well, don't go hurtin' yourself!" Troy joked. I gave him a weak smile. "Hey, is this about tall, dark, and big?"

"What? Oh, no, I don't think so. I was just off in wonderland." I gave him another smile, one I hoped would be more convincing. Hey, fake it til you make it, right?

"Well, it's gettin' late and we have four miles to run, so let's get in and change. I hope Screamin' Mimi's will still be open after, because girl's got to eat," Troy said, getting out of the car.

"What's the point of running if you're going to eat pizza?" I asked as I walked to his front door.

"Because, duh, when you run before you eat it doesn't count as eating."

I raised my eyebrow at him and said, "Boy, I want to live in your reality."

I put my neon-pink running shorts on and paired them with a white racer-backed running shirt. We mainly ran at night because running during the day in Savannah was listed just under water-board torture in the book of cruel and unusual punishment. Well, maybe not. But it should be. It didn't really cool off, but at least there wasn't the sun to contend with.

I walked out to find Troy lacing up his sneakers. Troy

wore the exact same thing as me, but in neon green. Short shorts and all. I shook my head at him. "I swear, Troy, I am never taking you shopping with me again."

He looked at me with an innocent, I-have-no-idea-what-you're-talking-about look on his face. "Okay, I'll admit your ass looks way better in them than mine, but my legs look better. Oh my God, we could so be twins!"

I just stood there gaping at him. Then we both burst out laughing. Between gulps of air and hysterics I said, "Come on, fatty, let's go delete the pizza."

The path we ran along was about four miles total. We mainly stuck to a wooded area and looped back through town, passing right by the hotel Reid and Mitch were staying at. That had absolutely nothing to do with why we were doing this path versus another path. Well, that's what I told myself anyway. After a few quick stretches, we were off.

Like most times when Troy and I ran, we chatted about his flavor of the month and my lack thereof. He knew about my virgin status and teased me relentlessly about it.

"God, Delaney, how have you not let Mr. Tall, Dark, and Lickable in your panties yet? He's welcome in my panties any time. Well, he would be if I wore any."

"Ah, Troy, TMI!"

It was about then when I started to feel the small hairs on the back of my neck stand on end. I developed this sense that we were being watched. I looked over my shoulder as we jogged, surveying the area and peering into the woods.

I didn't see anything, but that didn't mean much. Maybe it was just me being oversensitive. The full moon was nearing and my powers tended to get a little restless when the full moon neared. I shrugged off the feeling and chatted with Troy, trying to enjoy the time with the only friend I had. I could not keep my eyes from darting off in just about every conceivable direction.

"What in the hell are you looking for? Because if it's a man, oh or a donut, I'll stop," Troy said.

I rolled my eyes at him. Although a donut sounded a whole lot better than pizza. "No, I don't know, I just feel like someone is watching us. Do you feel it?"

Still jogging, Troy seemed to think about the question for a moment before he said, "No. Maybe it's a witchy thing."

This weird feeling was putting me on edge and I had to rein in my power a bit to keep from shooting off sparks and jolts. We kept on our path and I tried to shake the unease.

"Hold up!" Troy said a bit breathlessly. "My shoe." I stopped and jogged in place, waiting on Troy to finish. I couldn't help but look at the wooded area we were running alongside. That's when I saw it. Deep in the wooded area, to the right of a large oak, was a pair of glowing green eyes. I froze. They looked identical to Reid's when he was a wolf. That feeling I had before was my power trying to tell me what I pushed off. We weren't just being followed, we were being hunted. *Shit.*

In a low, calm tone I said, "Troy get up. Not quickly. But,

get up." Even bent over his spine seemed to stiffen.

Through our friendship Troy may question me and mess around, but when it came down to it he trusted me. And now I hoped that was true because I needed him to trust me so we could both get out of this with our throats intact.

"Troy, Reid's hotel is only about a mile away from us. You need to run to the hotel and stay there," I said to him, never taking my eyes off the wolf's eyes. I could feel the sparks falling from my fingertips. I had never hurt someone intentionally with my power. Could I do this? I mean, if I needed to? Hell, that could just be someone's German Shepherd. Yup, and my middle name was delusional. I looked over at Troy and the fear on his face clinched it for me. Of course I could. I was not some weak human with no power. I was a fucking witch.

"D, I will not leave you alone with whatever it is. How do you know that's not Reid?" he stated the question I feared most. I swallowed the lump that seemed to make its way up my throat and settle there. The wolf's eyes looked just like Reid's. But these weren't his. I didn't know how I knew, I just did. The wolf walked a few paces closer to us. He was still cloaked in darkness, all but his glowing eyes.

Without taking my eyes off the wolf I said, "Troy, please, I cannot have what happened to Sierra happen to you." I began to pull my power from my core to my hands. It was slightly painful, as my focus was not as sharp as it could be, but I had to be ready.

"D, I am not—"

That's when the freight train hit me.

Pain exploded from my left collarbone and my breath left me with a whoosh as I hit the ground. I pushed my palms to the wolf on top of me and willed my power to leave my core. The only thought I had was to get this snapping-jawed snarling beast off and away from me and get Troy and I out of there. The wolf went flying off of me as though he had a bungee cord attached to his back. The air stank of burnt hair and blood. I was dazed. There was no fighting this thing with as little experience as I had. It was too goddamned fast. I felt strong arms lift me up off the ground. Black stars threatened to take over my vision.

"Oh my God, D! Are you okay? We need to run," Troy's frantic voice sounded muffled.

I tried to meet his eyes, but had a hard time at first. When I did see his eyes, there was a wild fear in them. I shook my head, trying to clear the ringing from my ears. I saw a crumpled form off in the distance. That form snapped me back into reality. Shit, yeah, we needed to run because that form was getting up for round two and I knew I did not have that many rounds left in me. No words were needed; we ran.

Panting and gulping precious air, I huffed, "We. Need to. Get to. Reid."

Troy turned his wild eyes to mine and said, "One mile?"

"Less than," I panted. That's when I heard the snarling. Shit. I couldn't spare the time to look behind me, but I picked up the pace.

I heard Troy do the same behind me. Then his muffled cries shocked me out of my panicked run. Troy was kicking the beast with all of his might, but he couldn't shake him off his left arm. *Oh hell, no, not Troy*. It was a light switch inside me. My core exploded.

My power sat in a well inside me, waiting to be tapped. I had never tapped my power like this before. Never have I felt the lightning to strong within me. It begged to escape any way it could. Once my core erupted, my vision changed. Everything went white. After a second, I saw the forms of Troy and the beast as black shadows. I panicked for a moment, not knowing what to do with such power. I let the lightning guide me.

I stretched my right hand out toward the beast and pulsed my power. A bolt of lightning went careening toward it. I managed to clip him on his right hind leg. I heard the beast yelp and then snarl at me. His eyes seemed to grow brighter with the rage and pain I knew a blow like that would cause. It would not be enough to injure him, but it drew his attention to me and away from Troy. I ran to him and said, "Troy, get up. I know it hurts like hell, but I can't touch you right now."

His eyes met mine and he flinched. I had no idea what I looked like in that moment but it must have been frightening. I knew I didn't look human because, well, I didn't feel human. I glanced down at my hand to see that sparks were falling from them and from my arms.

"Fuck me. Goddamn asshole. I am never running again. I'll be a fat queen for the rest of my life," Troy said as he struggled to get up. I wanted to go to him and help. I wanted to wrap my arms around him and sooth him and me. I clamped down on that feeling because right now I would not only hurt him, I would likely kill him.

The beast limped in front of me, pacing back and forth snarling. My heart was racing faster than I thought possible for me to still be standing. I couldn't make out the color of his coat as anything other than black because of the weird black-and-white vision. He started toward me and I flicked my hand out and another bolt connected with the ground in front of him, dusting him with dirt. I. Was. Pissed. I was not some weak child.

"I am done running!" I yelled at the beast. "You started this and I WILL end it." I could feel the sparks raining down my body. I knew I sounded half crazed, but I would not be a victim. The wolf seemed to realize I would cause him more pain than it would be worth. He ducked his head, turned, and ran off into the woods.

Oh, I don't fucking think so. I started after him, then froze as I remembered him biting Troy. *Troy is hurt.* I ran to Troy, who was cradling his arm. He took a few steps away from me.

I hung my head, stepped back, and said, "Sorry, are you okay?"

"Uh, I don't know. But, Jesus, you look like a human sparkler. You're amazing, and your eyes. Delaney, they are silver and sparking. I have never seen anything like it," he said shakily.

"I-I-I don't know, this has never happened. Let me rein this in and then we need to get to Reid's."

I focused on pulling the power back into my core. *God, it hurts like hell.* I actually screamed. I tried not to, but I couldn't help it. It felt like my blood had turned to acid and was burning its way through my body. My eyes were clenched shut, but I heard Troy running over. I put up a hand to stop him just in case he was going to touch me. I couldn't be sure I wouldn't hurt him.

"I'm good," I rasped. God, what a fucking lie. Every part of me hurt and I mean every part down to a cellular level.

"You look normal now," Troy said hesitantly.

I stood up on weak wobbly legs and opened my eyes. Everything had color again. I released a breath I hadn't been aware I was holding.

"Troy, we need to go."

"Agreed."

IT WAS THE LONGEST HALF MILE OF MY LIFE. BY THE TIME we got to the hotel and to Reid's room, I didn't have the strength to stand any longer. Slumped against the wall just across from Reid's door, I slid down it until my ass connected with the ground. I placed my arms on the tops of my knees and rested my head on my arms. I had never been so grateful to sit in my life. I had nothing left. I couldn't even knock on the freaking door. Troy, however, about beat Reid's door down.

"Keep your pants on, I am coming," Reid's muffled voice sounded beyond the closed hotel door. The chain on the door rattled just before it opened.

I raised my head to look at Reid, but only saw Troy from his most flattering angle, according to him anyway. My head felt like it would explode, and if I opened my eyes again it very well may have happened.

"Troy, what the hell happened to you?" Reid's voice sounded frantic.

"We had a run-in with some sharp and pointies. Now, if you don't mind, I'm coming in. She won't let me touch her."

"Holy hell!" Reid's voice sounded closer this time and a bit wild.

I lifted my head up slightly and cracked my eyes slightly to see him. I was blinded for a moment. I felt Reid's strong hands cradle my face. As he touched me I felt his body shudder.

"Damn, Delaney, you're packing quite a punch." The shudder I felt in him must have been because of my power slipping from me to him. God, I just felt so damned drained.

"Sorry." It came out more a squeak, but it was all I could manage.

"Don't be. You were right to make sure Troy didn't touch you." His caramel-colored eyes were sparkling. He was so beautiful. Hulking brute of a man that he was he was, so beautiful. "Honey, I'm going to pick you up and take you inside so I can look at you better." I felt his strong arms wrap around me. One slipped around my back near my shoulders and the other behind my knees. "Troy, get the door." He gently set me on the bed. Or what this hotel passed for a bed.

"Look at Troy first," I said just as Reid was about to mess with the bite on my collarbone.

Reid didn't take his eyes off me, but his jaw tightened and his lips went into a white line. I knew it wasn't what he wanted to do, but I would be fine. I'm a witch, for God's sake. Troy needed help. Reid got up and went to see Troy in the chair by the door.

"Honey boo-boo, I'm fine, but our girl over there did some amazing shit," Troy said.

"Hold on one second, Troy. Let me go get Mitch," Reid said.

I stared up at the ceiling. God, what a fantastic mess this is. My life was a disaster area. This seemed familiar. At least this time I wasn't covered in foam. I snorted, trying to stifle a laugh.

"Get pants on first," Reid said, coming over to the bed.

"Fuck me, what the hell happened?" Mitch asked as he entered the room. Clearly he had been in the shower, as his hair was wet and he was missing a shirt. Lord help me, the man was toned. I looked over to find Reid also did not have a shirt on. Where Mitch was slim with a toned body, Reid was slim yet ripped, rippled, stacked ... pick an adjective.

Mitch went over to Troy and picked up his arm. Troy winced in pain.

"Ouch! Shit!"

"It's not broken, but you're going to need stitches for sure," Mitch said, setting Troy's arm down on his lap.

I thought Mitch was going to Atlanta? My confusion must have shown on my face because Reid said, "He was just getting ready to go. Can you sit up?"

Reid put his arm under my shoulders and leaned so close to me I thought I felt his lips brush the tip of my nose. Even as beat up as I was, my stupid heart kicked up a notch. *Stupid body.*

"Yeah I think so," I replied.

"So anyone want to inform me what the hell happened?" Mitch cut in. It was Troy who went over everything. While he spoke, Reid's hands went over my whole body making sure I had not broken anything. Well, that's what I was telling myself, anyway. As he wandered to the back of my head I braced for pain, but was not braced for that amount of agony.

"Shit, damnit, Reid! That hurts!"

He smiled and moved to my collarbone. At some point he got a wet towel and when he brushed it over the wound I about punched him. "The hell did you put on that thing? Ice water?"

"Shh. Nothing broken. You might have a concussion and it looks like the teeth bounced off the bone without doing much damage." It was at that point when Troy described how I looked. Reid sat there listening to him and never looking away from me.

"A witch who controls lightning. Damn. I have never heard of that before," Mitch said, looking over at me.

I raised my hand in the air and said, "Yup, that's me. Weird as hell."

A flash of something flickered across Reid's face, but I didn't know what it was. The next instant his face was buried in my neck. My heart kicked right back up again. I heard him take in a deep breath. *Is he smelling me?* Oh for fuck's sake, I was just attacked and ran forty thousand miles. Of course I smelled bad; why the hell did he need to smell me? I flinched back, but with arms around me there wasn't far I could go.

"What the hell…"

"Mitch," Reid snapped.

"On it," Mitch answered as he gingerly picked up Troy's arm and sniffed it.

Next to my ear I felt Reid's warm breath as he whispered, "Trying to catch a scent." My pulse rushed and heat spiked low in my belly. I clinched my legs, begging them not to betray me.

"Ah," was the only response I could manage. *Sheesh, calm down, killer.*

I thought I felt a brush of his lips over my neck just under my ear as he pulled away. But, he didn't give me a wicked grin or anything. Clearly, my mind was going.

"Reid, it's the damndest thing, but I don't smell him. How is that even possible?" Mitch said.

"I have no idea, but I don't smell him either."

"I need to head to Atlanta. My pack will be meeting me there and I will be speaking rather persuasively to them to see if I can find out who Bill saw."

"Can you take me to the hospital on your way? I don't need my fabulous skin scarring," Troy asked of Mitch.

"Sure. Delaney, you're going to need to go too," Mitch said.

"Yeah, no, that's not going to work for me. Too many electrical devices in that place." I met Reid's gaze and he did not look amused.

"Delaney, you really…"

"I'm fine, really, look," I said as I got off the bed. I was hesitant to leave Reid's warmth, but if I wanted to clear my head from this, his arms was not the best place for me to be.

I raised my arms above my head and noticed that it really didn't hurt that bad. However, there was a fresh trickle of blood forming down my shirt. I put my arms down to see all three men looking at me. Troy just shook his head.

"You big bastards better forget it. She's made up her mind. That's all there is to it. Also, are all werewolves as fine as y'all? Because that's right sinful." Ah, there it was. The reason Troy and I were friends. I couldn't help but chuckle.

Reid was still glaring at me when he said, "Fine. I'll take Delaney home and, Mitch, if you can drop Troy off."

I walked over to Troy and helped him out of the chair. I wrapped my arms around his narrow waist, being careful of his arm. He wrapped one lanky arm around me and we both just stood there holding each other. I refused to cry. I felt Troy press his lips to the top of my head.

"I love you. Thanks for saving my ass." Troy's voice sounded about as shaky as I felt. Damn, a tear slipped out. Stupid adrenaline let down.

I looked up at him and moved my hands to his face and said, "I love you too. Thanks for not leaving." I put my lips to his cheek and felt the skin was damp.

DELANEY HAGEN
ELEVEN

"**R**EID, YOU DON'T NEED TO COME UP. REALLY, I'M good." I really didn't need him to come up. Well, I mean not to keep me safe.

"Delaney, it's not up for discussion." There was an edge of desperation to his voice. It stopped the argument from falling from my lips. I simply stepped aside and let him in.

I needed Tylenol; my head was killing me. I had never used that much of my power before. I stopped in the middle of my living room when the tone of Reid's last comment fully hit me. It was laced with worry, worry for me. I had almost died. I could have gotten Troy killed. The enormity of the situation had been lost on me until this moment. One thought kept playing in my head over and over and finally when I saw Reid's expression I understood what it was saying. I would have never seen Reid again. I would have never felt my heartbeat race at his touch. I would never see what we could be.

We both stood there in my living room with our eyes locked, both trying to read the other. But, one thing was clear: we were at a precipice. In this moment, we had a chance. We had a choice. Do we stay the course or do we leap? My mind was racing, but my heart leapt.

"I could have died," I said, staring at his caramel-colored gaze. A shiver ran the length of my spine. That gaze seemed to strip me bare.

"I know." His voice was full of emotions. I just couldn't tell what they were.

Turn or leap? Now or never? Was it worth the risk of losing my heart? I ran to him just as he ran to me. We cleared the distance in two steps. His hands cupped my face and he crushed his lips to mine. It was a bruising kiss, one that would undoubtedly leave my lips swollen. One of his hands slipped from my face to the back of my head, where he tangled it in my hair. There was a sense of desperation in his kiss. He needed this just as much as I did. I slipped a hand to the back of his neck and ran my finger through the short hairs. His tongue flicked my lip and I met it with my own flick. Suddenly, he pulled away. He leaned his forehead against mine. We both gasped for breath.

"I don't want to hurt you. But, I need you, Delaney," he said in a growl.

My heart did this little flip-flop thing. He said he needed me. I don't think any man has ever said he needed me and if he did, he didn't say it with the conviction Reid just did. He said it as though he needed me like he needed oxygen in his lungs. I moved my head to look at him and my breath caught at the desire emanating from his gaze.

I swallowed and moved my hands to his face and whispered, "I'm tougher than I look."

That was all that it took before his mouth covered mine in a soul-searing kiss. His hand fisted in my hair so he could control the angle of my face to his. His tongue darted in and out of my mouth, mimicking other, more erotic activities. My belly tightened and heat rushed to the juncture between my thighs and began to pool. My body was remembering what almost had been. Remembering what his mouth felt like on my breast.

It was him who broke the kiss. He stared down at me and his gaze had no caramel color to be seen. The eyes staring back at me were the blazing green of the wolf.

He dipped his mouth to the base of my throat. His tongue flicked out, teasing and lapping at the sensitive skin. My hands flew to cradle his head closer to my throat. I felt his fingers circle to my lower back and then, in a fast move, he grabbed my ass with both hands and lifted me up. Instinctively, I wrapped my legs around his waist. His mouth never left my skin as he walked me over to my bed and set me down. He then took my shoes off and in a low tone said, "Stand up. On the bed." *Oh God, he isn't going to stop now, is he?*

I complied and stood on the bed. He walked over to me and placed his hands on my hips, running a finger along the waistband of my shorts. My breathing began to quicken and became erratic. He folded the hem of my shirt up, exposing about six inches of my belly. He began to lick and nip at the smooth skin. I ran my hands through his soft hair, trying desperately not to fall and look like a total nut case. His hands pushed my shorts down. And there I stood in my light-blue, lace hipster panties. My heart tried to beat right out of my chest. I knew my panties were damp and I knew he knew it.

He ran a finger along my wet heat. I gasped at his touch. I would fall, I just knew it. For a few agonizing moments he ran a finger over me, causing me to go even wetter, a thing I did not think possible. I looked down at him to see him watching me. He smiled as he placed his finger in his mouth and sucked it. My mouth became far too dry.

He withdrew his finger and said, "I cannot wait to taste you."

Sweet agony. I might explode. Words? A response? My brain had left the building. His mouth covered my heat and I felt him taste me through my sopping panties. *Oh God.* Pleasure spiked through me in a burst at that taste.

"Reid." It was a whisper, mostly breath, as my voice was becoming as elusive as my brain. "I'm going to fall." I felt him flick his tongue against my now-soaking panties before he lowered me to the bed.

He sat back on his heels, looking at me. There was so much in his expression and I got the sense that he was giving me this chance to back out, but that this was the only chance I would be given. I pulled my shirt the rest of the way off, only wincing a little at the wound on my collarbone. Reid pulled his shirt off as well and he hovered over me, staring at my body.

"God, Delaney, you are something."

I reached up to pull his face to mine and kissed him with all the need I felt for him. I let my hands wander over his muscular chest as he hovered above me. I felt his groan build in his chest.

He broke away from me, leaving my lips cold and aching for him. His lips scattered little kisses from my chin down my neck and to my breasts. My nipples were distended at the mere thought of his mouth. He licked the pebbled flesh, but didn't suck it in. I arched my back at him, hoping he would, but he only licked and then blew cold air. The moment the air hit my nipple, I sucked in a breath. He moved to my other nipple, doing the same. I felt his fingers circling my right nipple then his other hand trailed small patterns down my belly to the edge of my panties.

I stopped breathing as his hand slipped under my panties and his fingers slipped around my wet folds. I could feel something building inside me. He found my clit and began rubbing it, then slipped to my entrance, yet he never pushed inside me. I was dying. I might spontaneously combust.

Poof, gone never to be seen. But, oh God, what a way to go!

"Reid, please." I was not above begging him.

"No, I want to taste you first. I want to taste you as you come." His voice was just as ragged as mine was.

His hand left my sex and in that moment I wanted to cry in frustration. His mouth covered my left nipple and he drew the peak into his mouth. Gone was my cry of frustration, replaced by a cry of shock and pleasure. He withdrew me from his mouth and kissed his way down my body. He took his time nipping, sucking, and licking me. His fingers were rubbing small circles on my hips the whole time. He expertly pulled my panties down, leaving me fully naked in front of him.

"You are the most beautiful thing I have ever seen. I just can't get enough of you." His voice was laced with such raw need it made my body arch toward him.

He positioned himself between my legs and kissed each of my inner thighs so slowly it left me begging for more. Then I felt his tongue dipping into my liquid heat. I gasped his name and moaned it at the same time. My mind had gone long ago and I was simply swimming in what this man did to me and how he made me feel.

The pressure built and then I felt his finger slide inside of me. I tried to control my actions, but at the feel of his finger inside me, my hands flew to his hair. He found my clit and sucked it in. With one more flick of his tongue my orgasm hit me and what was left of my mind splintered and flew apart into a thousand pieces. He kept licking me and nipping at my sensitive nub. I may not have any experience in the sex department, but I have only been a one orgasm kind of girl.

"Reid, I can't..." I was cut off by the feel of him moving up my body.

He kissed my nose and said, "Oh yes, you can, and you will."

With his lightning speed he stood up and stripped off his pants in one motion. His erection was huge, his testicles drawn up tight. I knew it would hurt as he stretched me. But, the burn would be more than welcomed. I could not take my eyes off of him. I licked my lips as my mouth watered, wanting to taste him too.

I moved to the edge of the bed and scooted myself level with his mouth-watering erection. I ran my hand down the length of him and heard him hiss. I smiled up at his intense gaze. He had stopped breathing, waiting on my next move. I brought him to my lips and licked the head of him before drawing him fully into my mouth and suckling him. His hand fisted in my hair. He moaned and pulled away from my grasp, leaving me blinking up at him. Was I that bad?

"Christ, woman, you're going to undo me," he rasped as he climbed over me.

I spread my legs to accommodate him. He rested his erection against the wet, aching part of me. He leaned in to cover my mouth with his and began a slow grinding of his erection against my clit and my slick folds. The pleasure began to build, but the peak was out of my grasp. I wanted him inside me. Hell, I needed him inside me.

I arched up to meet him thrust for thrust. I wanted him to feel the same agony. His eyes met mine and I could tell he was in as much pain as I was in. Good. I broke our kiss. I sucked and licked my way down his neck and bit down hard on the tendon between his shoulder and throat. He gasped and let loose a moan that sent my head spinning. I then moved my hands to his back and dug my nails in as he ground his hard erection against my clit. He moaned again. That's when I felt his subtle shift and felt the pressure of him at my entrance. He pushed inside of me. White-hot pain laced up from my sex and flooded my body. He paused and searched my eyes. He must have seen the pain on my face, because his eyes were full of concern.

I put my hand against his cheek and said, "I want this. Please don't stop."

"Are you? I mean, have you ever?" he breathlessly questioned.

"Please, Reid!" I begged. If he stopped now I would electrocute him.

He closed his eyes. Clearly he was having some kind of internal struggle. I arched my hips up, pushing him in a fraction of an inch more. It was enough to show him how much I needed him. He pushed more into me and the pain burned, but it felt so damned good at the same time. He withdrew a little and then in one thrust was inside me fully. I cried out at the intrusion, but the pain was quickly replace with pleasure. If there had been a barrier there, it was long gone.

He began to move inside me. He withdrew and thrust inside all the way to the root. When he was inside me, he filled me all the way, and when he left me I felt empty and aching for him. I was a big ball of need and met his thrust with one of my own. I felt my orgasm building. His mouth left mine and went to my breasts, sucking and nipping at each nipple. He was going to make me burst. I just knew it. I needed to come so badly. He leaned up slightly and slipped his hand between us and found my clit with his thumb, rubbing it. With his touch pleasure shot through my body. With every beat of my pulse it sent the pleasure deeper into my core. Building, everything was building. I had never felt anything like it.

"God, Delaney you're so tight. I want to feel you come."

And just like that, as if my body needed him to say it, I came. I threw my head back and moaned his name. I felt him shudder and pulse inside of me and that only seemed to fuel my orgasm, stroking it to a fever pitch. For the second time today, I flew apart into a thousand pieces. I felt like a crystal ball falling to the earth, shattered into a million shards. I was raw and this man had done it to me. Completely exposed, soul and all.

I lay there with Reid on top of me as the after-quakes

of the monumental orgasm washed over me in waves. Reid brushed his mouth over my skin in light kisses, leaving my sensitive skin tingling.

I closed my eyes, just focusing on feeling him on me, in me, and around me. This male broke me down to the most elemental and base level. Any barrier I erected to keep him from getting to me he demolished. Here I lay, a quivering mess of raw nerves completely and utterly exposed. Yet, the feeling of vulnerability that I knew would come with being this exposed was nowhere to be seen. I felt safe. I had no idea that this feeling of panic and uncertainty had taken such a toll on my entire being.

"Oh, Delaney, you're bleeding," Reid said as he rolled off of me. His voice startled me out of my thoughts. I sat up without opening my eyes and my forehead connected with Reid's chin.

"Ouch! Shit, Reid, I'm sorry," I said, reaching to feel the knot on my forehead, but in doing so I whacked Reid's chin, again. *Oh sweet hot sauce I am a mess.* "Oh God."

"Woman, don't move before you give me a black eye." There was not an ounce of hurt or annoyance in his expression. There was, however, a glint of amusement in his gaze.

"I'm sorry. I'm such a mess," I said. Then I caught the red spot forming on his chin and winced.

"You're just enough mess. Now, sit up let me look at your shoulder." I sat up and stayed as still as possible. His touch was light as he looked over the wound.

"It's not as bad as I thought was," he said as he placed a light kiss on the skin just north of the wound. And, just like that, my heart kicked up a gear and began to thunder. He must have sensed the reaction I was having because he kissed me deeply. I pulled away and placed a hand over his lips as he came toward me for another kiss that would surely kick thing up another notch.

"Wait, let me go wash my collarbone off and get a few Band-Aids." He quickly nipped my finger and shifted fully off me.

I ran off to the bathroom as not to be naked for too long. Yes, the man and I had just done some intimate things, but it was plain weird to walk around nude with someone else in my home. I cleaned myself up from our activities then turned the faucet on and splashed some water over the wound. After it was cleaned off, I saw it was just a bite. I would have thought the were would have ripped at it or gone for my throat. *That's weird. Had he been trying to kill me?* If so, he was clearly the worst werewolf on the planet. Had he not been trying to kill me, then why attack? It made no sense. I found a few Band-Aids and placed them over the largest punctures. I found a white tank top that I slept in the night before and slipped it on. I also slipped on my black lace thong. Hey, it was all I had and would have to do until I found some shorts. Reid sat up against the headboard of my bed. He had no shirt on, and God, the sight of him made my mouth water and made me want to run my tongue down every part of him. I looked up to his face to find him smiling at me.

"You're looking at me like I'm dessert," he said, grinning even bigger.

I scoffed and said, "No, I'm just looking for shorts." I turned around and began looking through the basket on the floor. I heard a groan from the bed.

"Don't bother. It's more I'm going to have to take off of you." His tone was full of promise. I stood up and turned around and I knew my face had to be beet red because I totally forgot I had a thong on. I just mooned him. Ugh.

"Come here before I tackle you where you stand." I smiled and slowly climbed up the bed. I made my way to him, crawling up his body, and stopped when I sat straddling him. I wrapped my legs around him, bringing us pelvis to pelvis and that when I felt him hard and ready against me. *Holy hot sauce, batman, but this man is inexhaustible.*

"Reid, I don't think I can…"

"Not now. But, later. Right now I want to hold you. Wait, is that Hello Kitty?"

I looked down at my Band-Aids and sure enough they were. "Yeah, Troy…" I trailed off at the feel of his hand slipping under my shirt to draw circles on my back.

"I don't think the were was trying to kill me." His hand stilled at my words.

"No, I don't think so either."

"There's something we are missing. I just wish I knew

what it was." I knew there was something I needed to tell him, I just couldn't put my ... Oh, Mil! I then in great detail explained everything that Mil told me, including the prophecy. He was so still; I sat back slightly to see his face. He looked angry.

"Reid?" I questioned lightly. God, I knew I should have told him. I just didn't trust my gut. I let fear rule my actions and look where that had gotten me, a pissed-off werewolf.

"Delaney, why didn't you tell me?" He sounded so hurt. It hurt my heart to hear that tone.

"I guess I thought it was so absurd I didn't think it was relevant." *And I didn't trust you*, I didn't say.

I couldn't meet his eyes. This was the same fight we had three weeks ago in reverse. *Dammit, I suck.* "I guess I thought it wasn't true so there would be no reason for me to worry about it."

Reid put a finger under my chin, forcing my gaze to his.

"Listen, just because we think this prophecy thing is shit doesn't mean some psychotic prick out there doesn't believe it's real." His tone was firm and his eyes steady. God, I hadn't even thought of it that way. I thought this prophecy was bullshit, so I never thought someone would really believe in it. *I really am a moron.* I was so stupid, that's what this whole thing was about. I shifted off of Reid's lap. I needed to think and being so close to him made things all foggy. He reluctantly let me go. I scooted off the bed and began to pace.

"What are you doing?" Reid raised an eyebrow in question.

"I'm baking a fucking cake. I'm pacing. I think I'm having a revelation." I kept pacing.

"By all means, keep pacing. Your ass in those panties is making my mouth water."

His remark only made me falter slightly. This attack wasn't about killing me. I think that's pretty clear. This whole time the prick was killing witches knowing they were powerful, but he may not have taken the time to find out what all of their powers were. According to the prophecy, I did look like the likely person, as my powers to control lightning have never been seen before. What did Mil say, the God of Thunder made a child from his storm? Or some craziness. *Oh shit, and there it is. Why didn't I see it before?* I stopped pacing and turned to Reid.

"Reid, it was a test."

"What do you mean?"

"The attack tonight was a test. I think he wanted to find out what powers I had." Reid sat in bed, unmoving. He was giving what I said serious consideration. After a few heartbeats I saw when what I said sunk in and he realized what I was saying.

"Holy shit, Delaney, we are close! We have to be. That would be the only reason this asshole even knows about you. I didn't hear of any attacks on the other witches. He must know we are closing in and he wants to be sure he has it right this time."

"He knows I am his last chance," I said, knowing it was true. It had to be true. It was the only thing in this whole messed-up situation that made any sense. He sprung out of bed and grabbed his pants, and was shoving a foot in when he looked at me questioningly. "What are you doing, big guy?"

"We have seven, no, six days to get this guy," he said, buttoning his pants and making his way to the door of the apartment. I didn't stop him. He'd be back.

I heard the door to the apartment open. "Shit." Then I heard the door shut.

I stood by the foot of the bed with my hands on my hips, tapping one foot.

"You let me get all the way to the door without reminding me it's the middle of the night?" Reid said, coming toe to toe with me.

I looked all the way up his bare chest to his handsome face and smiled shyly. "I knew you'd be back."

He placed his hands on either side of my neck and put both thumbs under my chin, angling my face to his. "Delaney, we have six days to figure out who this guy is. I will not risk you in this." He moved a thumb to my lips, tracing each curve. I parted my lips slightly and kissed his thumb.

"I know. I don't want to risk you either. But tonight, let's just focus on us." After the words left my lips I knew that's what I wanted too. I stood on my tiptoes and guided his face to mine. We stood there just kissing, tasting, and learning each other.

"Let's get in bed, Delaney," he said, panting. He stripped off his pants, revealing just what he wanted to do in that bed. I began to take my top off when he said, "No, keep it on."

Oh God, was I wrong about his intentions? I felt heat rush to my face in embarrassment.

"Sorry, I…"

"Hush," he said, covering my mouth with his in a brief kiss. "I want it off, but I want to be the one to take it off." He sat on the edge on the bed and pulled me between his legs. He slowly lifted my shirt up over my head and tossed it to the floor.

REID JAMISON
TWELVE

DELANEY'S SKIN LOOKED LIKE A MIX OF CREAM AND honey. Her skin felt like heated silk. I traced along the line of her spine. Even in her sleep she shuddered at my touch. Just this little bit of her exposed, her naked back made my cock twitch. She had been a virgin at twenty-six. *How does that even happen anymore?* Well, I guess it wasn't that surprising, mainly because she had been slipping mild bolts of electricity through me all night.

I placed a kiss at the base of her spine above her luscious ass just before I slipped out of bed. I needed to make a quick call to Mitch and clue him in to how close we were to nabbing this guy. I needed to get Mitch back down here so we could put pressure on him and see if we could force him into making a mistake.

I crept to my discarded gray athletic shorts laying on the floor. I slipped them on and turned to view the sleeping form on the bed. God, she was beautiful even when she slept. I slinked to the front door and slipped out.

"Saldana." Mitch sounded out of breath. But, over a phone, who really knew.

"Mitch. It's Reid, you need to get your ass down here."

"Reid," he said in a steady tone, "you are not my alpha. You do not give me orders."

Whoa. The fuck was that? He knew outside of this case I had nothing over him, as I did not want to be in a pack, nor did I have some delusion of grandeur of taking over one.

He went to Atlanta to see if one of his pack had betrayed him. I was guessing that's why he was on edge. I had never been in a pack much less dealt with the headache that was being an alpha. So, I had no idea what he was dealing with. But, I would kin it to a family member betraying him. That thought softened my tone.

"Mitch, I apologize, but I do need you down here. Did you figure anything out up there?" My tone was as even as I could manage, as my temper was always hot despite rationality.

"I'm sorry. It's been a long-ass night. No, I had a few pack members who did not show up so I hunted them down, questioned them, and they are being punished for their disobedience. But other than that, unless they are lying I didn't turn anything up." I heard whimpers and whines in the background. "What's up? Why do I need to be in a burning hurry to get back there?"

"I had a conversation with Delaney. She relayed a ton of information she learned from her great aunt."

"You gonna make me beg?"

I went on to tell Mitch everything Delaney told me about the witch history and the prophecy. I then explained how we thought this guy was testing Delaney and how we thought we might be closing in on him.

"Christ, Reid, you discovered all of this last night and are just now calling me? What the hell was so damned important you couldn't call me?" He sounded so hurt.

I was fucking Delaney within an inch of her life. I had some Earth-moving and soul-shattering sex with Delaney. Yeah, I didn't think any of that would really work as an appropriate response. Clearly while I was trying to come up with something, anything, to say, I left the line in silence for too long.

"Reid? You didn't," Mitch said.

This was not like me. I did not just hop into bed with someone, much less someone involved in a case I was working on.

"Damnit, Reid! You better not let this interfere with getting this asshole. And I was going to ask her out."

The thought of Mitch taking Delaney out made me want to punch something. Mitch and I had been friends for some time, but I did not want him anywhere near Delaney. It was not that I thought something would happen between them. It was the wolf; clearly he was being pulled toward Delaney despite my misgivings about the situation. I liked her quite a bit. But, putting myself out there to get hurt, I just didn't think that was something I could do, not right now. Well, if that was true then I wouldn't care if he did anything with her. And yet here I am about to break the phone because of the thought of him asking Delaney on a freaking date.

"Mitch, just get down here. And don't think about asking for details. I know you were about to," I said in an even tone.

"You're no fun at all. I'll leave here in about an hour. So, I'll be there in five hours. I say let's go see her aunt. Maybe she knows more about this than she told Delaney." I heard a car door shut and an engine start up.

"Yeah. We have six days. Mitch, we cannot let this guy get Delaney."

"Agreed." The call was disconnected with that.

My head was honestly reeling with thoughts of Delaney. *How do I feel about her? Do I love her?* My body thought I did, but my head was trying to talk some sense to my heart before it leapt out of my chest. Would my life be empty without her in it? Yes. I knew I felt strongly for Delaney. Now I just needed to figure out what to call this emotion.

I snuck back into the apartment to wake Delaney, who was still asleep. Every bit of me wanted to crawl up beside her and nuzzle her neck. I walked over to her face and knelt down to kiss her nose. She didn't ever stir. Damn, the girl could sleep. I pushed her brown hair out of her face and stroked her cheek.

"Delaney, it's time to get up. We have work to do."

She groaned and flipped over, giving me a complete view of her naked back and ass. Christ, this woman had power over me that no woman should have. My cock jumped to attention without consulting my brain. I couldn't help myself. I grabbed her soft flesh. She let out a soft moan.

"Reid, not again, or I won't be able to walk," she said sleepily.

"Then you better cover your ass because," I said, squeezing her ass harder, "I am having a hard time concentrating."

With that she rolled over and blinked up at me. Her lips were slightly puffy and her eyes were a bright storm-cloud gray. She looked like she had been thoroughly fucked. The thought made me smile.

"Why are you smiling?" she asked, reaching for my lips with her thumb.

Nipping at her thumb, I said, "Because you look good enough to eat. And if you don't get out of that bed, you're going to be what's for breakfast."

"Not the best motivation, but I'll get up."

When she got up she was completely nude. And my God her body could make a dead man twitch. All I could do was stare at her as she walked over to me. She flung her arms around my neck and pressed her lips to mine in a firm kiss. I kissed her back with interest, the feel of her naked breasts against my naked chest sending blood rushing to my cock. *Ugh,* this was not helping my motivation to get this day started and it was already after 10 A.M. She pulled away as though she knew we needed to stop before we ended up back in that bed.

"I'm going to take a shower then get dressed. Will you make some coffee for me? I fear if I invite you in we won't leave." She turned and sashayed her pretty little ass to the bathroom. I had a sneaking suspicion she wiggled it a little more just for me.

About twenty minutes later she came out with wet, slicked hair. She wore short jean shorts with a white lace tank top and under that tank top was a light-blue spaghetti-strapped shirt. The hem of that shirt ended about three inches shy of her waistband, showing three inches of lace-covered skin. This female was a man's wet dream. I handed her a mug of coffee.

"Well, what do we do today? I feel like we need to put the pressure on," she said, breathing in the scent of her coffee.

"Mitch should be here in about four hours. How about you call up your aunt and see if we can drop by. I think that is going to be the best place to start."

"Did he find anything with his pack?"

"No, but I think we need to focus on this area and protecting you."

With that last bit she choked on her coffee. I knew she would be pissy over that last one.

"What? Why? I do not need a babysitter," she said indignantly.

"No, you need someone around just in case. You will be with myself or Mitch at all times." Mitch with her, yeah, that was not going to happen. "Preferably me."

She raised her eyebrows at me and smiled. "A tad jealous, are we?"

Hell fucking yes I am. But, I sure was not going to admit that to her. "Maybe."

She set her coffee cup on the table and crossed her arms over her chest. She looked cute when she was gearing up for a fight. Her lips set in a hard line and her brow was pinched.

"Reid, what are we? I mean, what is this?"

The question hit me like a ton of bricks. I honestly did not know what to say. Did I want a relationship with her? Did I want to claim her? Was she my girlfriend? A girlfriend. The thought made me shudder. How the hell did I answer that question? I could love her. I looked into her searching gaze. There was variability there. This question was important to her and it was to me.

"Delaney, let's just take it day by day. I enjoy being with you. We do not need to label this." While that was the truth, it felt wrong to say. I felt like I was lying.

Her face was absolutely unreadable. For a few heartbeats we both just stood there staring at each other. Did I want her to have a reaction? *Ugh!* I was like a teenager with this woman. I had no idea what I wanted.

"I'm going to call Mil and tell her to expect us." She turned her back to me.

I was such a shit head. Could I not just say, *I really care for you*? Hell I may love you. How hard was that? But, no, I let her walk away. *Such a chicken shit*. I shook my head in self-disgust.

"Hey, Mil. Are you up for having guests? I thought I would bring a few friends by…" There was a pause. "Yes, Mil, I'll think about moving. We should be there in about five hours." Pause yet again. "Oh okay, bye."

"Everything okay?" I wondered.

Delaney wrinkled her brows at the phone then looked up to meet my gaze. "Yeah, she said she would be there, but had to go because the carpet cleaner was at the door." We both just stood there looking at each other and then without any words spoken we busted out laughing.

"She's getting her…" Delaney spoke between gulps of air and sobs of laughter. "…Her carpet cleaned."

"What are we, seven?" I said, having a hard time halting my own laughter. Finally, after the laughter calmed, I said, "Hey, let's go to my hotel room so I can get clothes. We can review the files to kill time before Mitch gets here."

Delaney gave me a smile and said, "Let's do this." But, there wasn't the spark of joy her smile normally held. And I was the one who did that. I was such an ass.

So we knew all of the witches that were killed were once registered, but at the time of death they were not. So, I would say the killer thought the witch he was looking for was once registered but no longer. None of this made sense because Delaney had never been registered. It seemed like this guy had a list and was just going down it one by one. It couldn't be that easy, could it?

"Delaney, how much do you know about the Coven?"

She put the file she held on the bed and thought about the question before she answered it. "A fair amount, why?"

"Do they have a record of all of the witches who were once registered and now no longer are?"

"I am one hundred percent sure they do. The Coven keeps meticulous records. If the Coven is anything, they are all up in people's business. That's why Mil and I moved so much. The Coven's reach is impressively intense."

Shit. I tried to calm my tone with my next question. "When we first met you were shocked the Coven hired me to look into this, why?"

She honestly looked taken off-guard with the question. "Two reasons." She held up two fingers. "One, the Coven tends to handle their own issues. I have never known them to look outside the Coven to solve an issue. I guess this one was so big they needed help. And two, they have never once cared about unregistered witches. Why would they start now?"

Shit. Those fucking bastards. They knew. I threw the files nearest me across the room. They made me sick to even look at. Delaney got up and walked over to me. She reached out to stroke my cheek, but before she could touch me I grabbed her hand and kissed her fingers.

"Reid?" she said in a concerned voice. "Are you planning on enlightening me?"

"Delaney, the Coven knew not only about the prophecy, but they knew the information had to have come from inside the Coven itself. They knew all of this, yet did not tell me any of it."

Delaney plopped down next to me.

"Do you think they thought the prophecy had nothing to do with this? Maybe that's why they didn't tell you?" Even her tone said she didn't believe that. I gave her a look that told her what I really thought of that question.

"Yeah, I didn't think so either." She grabbed my hand and laced our fingers together.

The gesture was strangely intimate. I had not held a woman's hand since Beth. It felt right. Like I was where I was supposed to be.

"What now?"

"We go see your aunt. Then I think I need a meeting with the Coven."

Delaney's brow furrowed and I could tell she didn't like my last comment. This female had so much fight in her it's no wonder she had control over lightning. She was so much like her element. She looked as though she was gearing up for a fight so, before she had a chance, I claimed her mouth with mine.

I was jolted out of my fogged brain by the sound of someone clearing their throat. Clearly, I was deafened by my pounding heartbeat because I did not hear the door open.

"Sorry, did I interrupt? Because I could have sworn we had a job to do," Mitch said in a clearly annoyed tone. Wait, not just annoyed, he looked pissed. His tone riled the wolf in me. *Calm down, big guy. He wants to catch the guy as much as you.*

"Sorry, you're right. You ready to go, Delaney?"

She stood up eye both of us and nodded.

The drive to Delaney's aunt's house took about an hour. The whole way, she looked restless. She couldn't sit still to save her life and it was driving me insane.

"What is wrong with you?" The question came out with more bite that I anticipated.

"Oh, sorry, I just feel funny. Like a disturbance in the force. I can't really explain it. Just ignore me," she said, continuing to shift around in her seat. "Hey, why didn't we drive in the same car? I mean, you and Mitch never seem to drive in the same car. That's weird."

"Because of you. Two unmated males in the same space with an unmated female can make us a little testy and make the situation dodgy."

"What does it mean to be mated?" she asked, not meeting my eyes.

I explained all about what it means to be mated and claimed. She seemed to only become more agitated at my words. Her eyes were becoming incandescent and her scent, which was normally gardenias and ozone, was sharpening with more ozone than normal.

"Please pull over," she whispered. I couldn't understand what was going on with her so I did as she asked.

As I pulled off the road I looked at her more fully. She had beads of sweat on her brow and rolling down the side of her face. Her eyes were pinched closed and her fists were clenched in tight balls. I had no idea what she was going through, thus I had no idea how to help her. I reached out to put my hand on her cheek when her head snapped to me and her eyes popped open. Gone was the happy, spunky girl. All that was behind her eyes was lightning.

DELANEY HAGEN
THIRTEEN

I HAVE NEVER HAD THIS HAPPEN BEFORE. FROM THE moment we started this drive, my power had felt so uneasy. I didn't know what was happening, but I couldn't control it. Reid reached out to touch me; I could sense it and did not want to hurt him.

"Reid, I need to get out of the car for a moment. Can you please click my seatbelt and come open the door? I don't want to hurt you." I had to manage my breathing because my voice was shaking.

"Can you tell me what's going on?" His own voice was steady, as though he were talking to a skittish deer. He leaned over and I tensed. *Please don't touch me.* I braced myself for his reaction to me when I heard a click and felt the release of the seatbelt.

"I-I-I don't know what's wrong. I don't have control of the lightning. I need to get out and find a way to control it or fry everything around me." I met his gaze around squinted eyes. My vision was going black and white, just like it did after the attack. I saw his nod, reluctant as it was, and squeezed my eyes shut. The slam of the door made me jump and I almost lost it. *What the hell is going on with me?* Something was wrong; I just didn't know what it was. I felt the door to my right open and I eased outside without opening my eyes.

"Please give me a few seconds." I opened my eyes and walked about fifty feet away and laid on the ground. Distantly I heard Mitch's door open and heard their voices, but couldn't make out what they said. *Okay, let's get this shit together.*

I focused on my core and tried desperately to pull my power toward it. The lightning wanted out, and it wanted out now. I sat up and looked around until I found a tree. I stood up and sprinted the hundred or so feet to the small oak tree, kicking up dust and rocks as I ran. I was so desperate to get this power settled. It felt like something was calling the lightning out of me. My heart was about to beat out of my chest. When I got to the tree I placed my hand on its broad truck and said through clenched teeth, "I'm sorry." I closed my eyes and let go of the control I held on the lightning.

The power left me in a rush, leaving me feeling dizzy and lightheaded. I heard a loud snapping noise and several popping noises. My nose was flooded by the scent of burning wood. *Oh shit! Did I start a fire?* I opened my eyes to see that I had someone how split the tree in half and the trunk was charred black in the center. I staggered back a number of steps and plopped down on my ass. *At least my power feels a little more settled, but man I still felt unsettled.* I had to see Mil. This was not normal.

I made my way back over to the car and just before I got there I heard the crash of the tree. I winced at the sound. Not just because of the loud noise, but because I had to kill a tree. I sent up a silent prayer and a vow to replace the tree as soon as I could.

"Doing some gardening?" Mitch's voice rang over the snaps of the tree.

I got to the door and Reid opened it. "Yeah, something like that," I replied in a clipped tone. I had no reason to be annoyed with him so before the door shut I yelled, "Sorry, let's just get there."

About twenty minutes later, we pulled up to Mil's house and I knew something wasn't right. I looked over to Reid, who just looked back with a questioning expression on his face. Without saying it, he was asking me what was wrong. How did I tell him something was wrong without seeming like a moron?

"I am just uneasy. Let's go in," I said, unbuckling my seatbelt. *Stop being crazy, Delaney! Calm your shit down and get a flipping backbone.*

The three of us walked up to the door and Mitch

knocked. I was between Mitch and Reid. *Talk about a beefcake sandwich.* The thought made me chuckle. Mil didn't come to the door. Mitch knocked again. My stomach sank to my feet and I had an awful feeling.

"Mitch, open the door. Something's wrong. If it's not open I know where the extra key..." I was frantic.

My heart was trying its best to beat right out of my chest. The door was open. She NEVER left the door unlocked. *Please, God, not Mil.* Tears were already filling my eyes. Mitch took a hesitant step in, and when I went to push past him Reid grabbed my arm. I felt his grip tighten and shudder. Clearly I had zapped him.

"Delaney, please wait. Let Mitch go first," he said, clearly concerned. Yeah, fuck that mess. I eased up for a moment until Reid's grip on me loosened. Then I bolted out of his hold and ran into the house.

"Damnit! Delaney!" I heard Reid bellow behind me. Honestly, I didn't care what he said. I just knew I needed to find Mil. And I needed to find her now. My eyes were darting every direction at once. I ran to the two small bedrooms. *Nothing, damnit; where are you, Mil?* I knew how wild I looked running through this house, because I felt just like the lightning within me, wild and out of control. I didn't know if I saved the kitchen for last because I knew she would be in there and I was delaying the inevitable or if I hoped what my power and body had been telling me was not true.

Mitch was standing in the doorway of the kitchen. He had a look of pity and horror plastered on his face. I couldn't see into the small room with him blocking my view.

"Get outta my way! MIL!" I punched him on the chest yet he remained. Tears were stinging my eyes and my throat began to tighten. I looked up to meet Mitch's gaze. His eyes were red and slightly puffy. With tears streaking down my cheeks I said, "Mitch I will blast you into next Sunday if you do not get out of my way." I meant every word of what I said. I began to pull energy from my core when he reached up with his thumb and wiped a tear from my cheek. He stepped aside and I staggered inside.

Mil lay on the floor in a small heap. I ran to her, tripping in my hurry. Tears were blurring my view of her. I had to find out what was wrong and fix it. That's right. I could fix this. All I needed to do was find out what was broken. I wiped at my eyes to clear my vision. There was no blood. *Did she have a heart attack?* I dismissed that thought as soon as it entered my head.

I brushed her soft silver hair from her neck and face and that's when I saw the purple and red bruises around her neck. *Shit!* I placed two fingers next on her carotid artery, waiting for a faint bump-bump. I felt only cool soft skin beneath me. I needed to start her heart. *Shit! How? I don't have a defibrillator. Holy fuck, you moron, you are a defibrillator!* I placed my hands on her chest just over her heart. I closed my eyes and took a small breath to steady my concentration. I pulled slightly on my core, sending my power out in a sharp quick pulse. I placed my fingers back on her neck and felt nothing. *Again!* I had to fix her! She was all that I had left.

Time stood still. I was deaf and blind to everything around me. It was just me. Time was of little consequence when my life was falling down around me. All I could do was scramble to pick up the pieces and hope none of the rubble consumed me. I honestly didn't know how long I sat there. I stopped because I could no longer pull from my core. My power was nothing more than a static spark. *I failed. What use am I to anyone?*

I plunged my face in her silver, lifeless hair and sobbed, falling apart completely. I cried what seemed like every tear I was born with. I cried until every part of me burned. I cried until all I could do was gasp for air. I lay on the floor next to the woman who was my mother after mine died. Maybe this was my punishment. My punishment for killing my parents. That had to be it. I didn't get tell her I loved her. I lay there on the cool laminate floor, praying for the pain to end. It hurt so much, this emptiness.

I felt a warm, strong hand slip beneath my head and one beneath my knees. He lifted me up to his warm chest. I tried to protest, but had nothing else to give. *I need to be here with Mil! I need to stay with her. What if she woke up?* I couldn't fight the man holding me. But, I refused to seek comfort from him. I didn't deserve it. I laid my head on his chest and felt first the steady bump-bump, bump-bump, bump-bump of his heart next to my ear. Then, sound began to penetrate my bubble. Now I could hear the steady beat of his heart.

"Delaney, can you hear me?" It was Reid's voice that reached me. I didn't respond. I didn't know how to form words without losing myself to the darkness that was growing inside me. I had this gaping hole forming where my heart should be. *Maybe I don't have a heart?*

"Delaney can you hear me? Are you okay?" Reid's voice again pierced the rushing noise taking over my hearing. Am I okay? What kind of question was that? Okay. What did that word even mean? I was breathing, Mil wasn't, nothing about that was okay. I tried countless times to open my eyes. Finally, after what seemed like an hour of trying, I did. I was looking up at the roof of Reid's jeep. I bolted up. *Where am I?* Had I been so out of it that he forced me to leave?

"Delaney, whoa, hold on, babe. Lay back down." Reid's voice sounded distant.

My head was spinning and my lips and eyelids felt swollen. I realized Reid was beneath me, my head on his lap. "Are we," I tried to speak, but the words came out as nothing more than breath. Reid brushed a few loose strands of hair away from my face. The heat from his fingers against my forehead left my skin tingling. I pinched my eyes shut then opened them. I tried six times to swallow the lump in my throat, but couldn't seem to manage it. I gave up and pushed my voice out in a rasp, "Are we still at Mil's?"

Reid met my eyes and his were full of such pain I felt a stab in my heart. Had he been hurt? He nodded in the affirmative. Good, I couldn't leave Mil. What if she woke up?

"What do I do now? I mean, how do I go on? Reid, I don't know if I can." I felt yet more tears roll down my cheeks.

Reid's thumb traced the path of my tears, drying the damp skin. "Delaney, I know you're in pain and, God, that hurts me more than you know, but we need to get this guy. I need you to hold it together, honey."

Hold it together. I wanted to laugh in his face. How? I was surprised I could remember to breathe. I couldn't help it. I started laughing. I was hysterical. I mean, whose life was I living? Hopefully not mine, because if it were, that would mean I was in such deep shit. Between whoops of laughter and gasps for breath I said, "Hold it together?" Yeah, okay.

"Delaney, Mitch has called the Coven to report her death. They will likely send someone to come collect her." He studied my face as the laughter died abruptly. The Coven was coming here? Why would they? *Shit*. She was in the inner circle before me.

I looked up to find green wolf eyes peering straight through to my bones. They should have scared me. They should have made me pee my pants and go running screaming to the hills. But, they grounded me. Like a slap in the face to bring me back to reality. "We need to get out of here," I said as calmly as I could.

I had to come to terms with the reality that Mil was gone. My world was sitting in piles of rubble at my feet. Now, I had to work on stumbling through the mess to what lay beyond it. I moved to the front seat of the car and Reid shifted to the driver's seat.

He started the car and pulled out of the driveway. "Reid," I said in a soft tone.

"Hmm?"

"Why is this happening?" I choked on the last word. My eyes began to burn with the need to spill tears. *God, get it together!*

"I-I don't know Delaney. I wish it weren't, but we will get this guy. I swear it."

The rest of the ride was spent in silence. What could I say? What could he say? The pain I had seen in his eyes was a very real pain. It was pain for me. Seeing me hurt had caused him pain. My stomach did a little flip-flop as the seed of a thought bloomed in my brain. I looked over at Reid, who just parked in my lot. His face had become a sight chiseled out of stone. I raised my hand and placed it on his cheek. At that moment I knew he was feeling powerless to help me, and Reid Jamison did not do powerless well. However, the effect of my touch was evident as his features softened.

"Come up with me?" It wasn't just a question, it was a plea. I needed him to come up to my apartment. I needed it for me, to get from one breath to the next. I would not beg him, but I needed him to know how much I needed him.

Oh God, I love him. I knew I loved him as surely as I could feel my heart beating. The realization made me a little light-headed with the merit of emotions I had crashing over me.

"Of course." His face softened further and he placed his hand over mine on his cheek. Did he know how I felt? Did he feel the same? I shook my head to clear it of all of the thousands of thoughts and feelings bombarding me. I gave him a weak smile and got out of the car.

I CRIED. AND WHEN I SAY I CRIED, I MEAN I UGLY CRIED. Snot, hiccupping, tears, and hyperventilating. Not once that night did Reid do anything other than let me express everything. I was an open wound that needed to breathe. Around 3 A.M. I rolled over in bed and looked to see if he was awake and of course he was.

"Are you okay?" It was a question I should have asked earlier, but was too bombarded by my grief to worry about.

"I have never been so powerless before, Delaney. I want to take the pain for you. I want to take the hurt and leave you nothing but the healing." He broke our eye contact to look down. "But I can't."

I was speechless. I slipped my arm under his head and shifted my body to mold to his. My body was made for his, I was sure of it. I fit so perfectly in his arms. It was then, with us holding each other, when I saw it. He needed me and my comfort as much as I needed it from him. There was nothing sexual or heated about our touching. His strokes along my skin were for simple reassurance that I was here. My strokes along his skin were for reassurance that not everything was a nightmare.

I closed my eyes and slept knowing three things. One, I loved Reid. Two, Mil was really and truly gone. Three, we had five days until the new moon. And we would kill this son of a bitch.

DELANEY HAGEN
FOURTEEN

IDREAMT ABOUT KEYS. ALL KINDS OF KEYS. SHORT keys, big keys, Victorian-style keys, locker keys, so many damned keys. I was drowning in a sea of keys, knowing I needed one of them. I woke up panting.

Reid yelled from the bathroom, "There's coffee on the table!" *Oh God bless him!*

"I had the weirdest dream. I was swimming in a sea of keys. Apparently, I was looking for one, but couldn't find it." I poured myself a cup of coffee and sat at the table.

Reid walked into the kitchen, clearly having just stepped out of the shower. The sight of him always sent my heart into an erratic rhythm. *I shouldn't be happy.* My heart shouldn't continue to beat; it should be a dead space in my chest.

"That is weird." Reid bent down and kissed me briefly. "What's even weirder is that when I put you in the car I went back to tell Mitch and saw Mil had something in her hand

and well…" He handed me a small silver key. On the top of the key there were four numbers. 1-8-7-6.

What the hell did this key and the dream mean? What was it to? Why did Mil have it? God, I had so many damned questions and no one to answer them.

"What do you think it goes to?" I questioned. I had no idea. For all I knew it could go to a locker at a roller rink.

"Let me see it." I handed him the key. He took it and flipped it over, glancing at the numbers and fingering the shape. "Looks like a key to a safety deposit box."

I stood up and snatched the key. I looked at it. Mil hated using a bank. She didn't even have a checking account. But, she had one account with one bank that she used to pay her rent. I ran to the door and threw it open. I felt a strong arm snake around my waist and haul me back.

"Hey! Let me go! I know where we need to go!" I tried to walk to the door, but my feet were no longer on the ground.

"Whoa there, killer. I am all for going to the bank, but maybe you should put some pants on. I mean, I love your ass, but I'm not too keen on others loving it like I do," he said, setting me down.

I looked down at my pale legs sticking out of the bottom of the huge T-shirt. *Shit!* I couldn't seem to remember pants lately. *What is wrong with me? I love pants. Shit, I love being fully clothed. Sheesh.*

"Oh, yes, well there is that," I said, darting off to the closet to dress.

I found a pair of loose-fitting jeans. They were a little big in the waist and hung on my hips. I matched them with a black racer-back top that had splashes of silver paint on it. Hey, at least it was all clean. I didn't have much time to do laundry lately. Mil used to come help me with it when I was behind. The thought of Mil caused a knife-like pain in my chest. I stopped in the entrance to the kitchen and plopped down to my ass. How could I continue like nothing happened?

"Delaney! Are you okay?" Reid ran over and knelt down to look at me.

"How do I go on? I have a thought about her and it hurts so badly. I don't think I can keep reminding myself to breathe, Reid." And cue the tears. Dammit. I couldn't seem to keep it together.

"Look at me." I met his caramel gaze. "From what you have told me Mil was like your mother. Pain is okay, Delaney. But falling apart isn't okay. She raised you to be a strong woman, not a weak thing. It's not about how we get there, Delaney; it's about the fact that we got there at all." His tone was so full of hurt, it hurt my heart just to hear him.

I nodded. Speech was an ability I did not possess at that moment. He was right, of course. This buttercup needed to suck it up and catch this guy. With Reid's help, I got to my feet. I wiped my tears with the back of my hand. I would not cry again. I could not give this asshole any more of my tears.

WELLS FARGO WAS THE ONLY BANK I KNEW MIL HAD even set foot in. She never went to the one nearest her house because she said she couldn't stand the people working there. She went to the one just a few streets away from my apartment. When I walked into the bank, I was blasted with frigid air. *God bless central air.* Reid said he would wait in the car to give me some time to handle whatever this was. I was greeted by a sharply dressed African-American man. He was about six foot tall and had a shaved head that resembled cue ball. His tie was a solid cornflower blue. His smile was infectious and made me smile despite the storm brewing inside me.

"Hi, there! I'm James. Welcome to Wells Fargo. How can I help you?" He spoke in a way that told me he seemed to really enjoy his job.

"Hi, James, I'm Delaney Hagen and my Aunt Mil…" I paused, trying to choke out the next words without bursting out into tears and becoming a blubbering mess. "…just passed away and she was found with this key. I thought maybe she had a safety deposit box." I handed him the key.

"Sure, let's step into my office and see if we can figure this out." Thankfully he didn't say anything about my puffy eyes.

We sat in his office while he typed on his keyboard. I had no idea how to deal with this kind of thing. I hated going into a situation not knowing anything. I began to pluck the frayed strings around a hole in my jeans.

"What was your aunt's name and address?" I gave him the information and waited for him to type it all in. "Can I have your license or ID?" I shoved my hand in my pocket and handed him the ID.

"Well, Ms. Hagen. Your aunt did indeed have a box here and you are the only one listed to be able to open it. You know, it's weird, she opened this box only a few days ago. Anywho, follow me and I will help you find the box."

A few days ago? I just stood there like a moron. Had she known this was going to happen? And maybe that's why she had opened the box? I guess she made the assumption that I would find the key. *Hell of an assumption, Mil!* I mentally chided. Maybe she had crazy dreams like I had. I shook my head to clear it of the millions of questions that were forming. I followed James into a room with a large vault door. Holy crap but there were a ton of little metal doors.

"I found it!" I yelled to James, who was looking on the opposing wall. I slipped the key into the latch and heard the telltale snick of the lock opening. I felt a hand on my shoulder and froze.

"I'll let you be, please let me know if you need anything." He squeezed my shoulder in a show of support and I almost lost it. All I could do was nod.

I pulled out a box about the size of a shoe box and set it on a long rectangular table behind me. I sat down and opened the box. In it was a single cream envelope with my name scripted on the front. I'm not sure what I was expecting, but this wasn't it. I mean, I didn't think there would be Blackbeard's treasure in here, but a letter? That's all?

I flipped the letter over and it had an honest-to-God wax seal on the back. In the seal was the mark of the Coven. I broke the seal slowly as to not destroy the wax, then slipped the letter out and unfolded it. It was Mil's handwriting for sure. I didn't get past *Delaney* before the tears sprang to my eyes. I would not do this here. I folded the letter back up and stuffed it in the envelope and nearly ran out of the bank.

I sat in the car and opened the letter. *"Delaney, I owe you more than a mere letter, but you need to know, I did not tell you everything..."*

"Hey, so what did Mil leave in the box?" I jumped at the question. I folded the letter up and stuffed it in my purse. I wanted to be alone when I read it. Clearly, Mil knew some things I didn't. Could she really have known this was going to happen?

"Just a letter. So what's the plan for today?" I couldn't meet his eyes. Sometimes I don't think I can meet anyone's eyes without seeing concern staring back at me.

"Well, I know you have things to deal with here. While you were in the bank I booked a flight to Dallas. I notified the Coven I would be there tomorrow morning. My flight leaves this evening. We have five days. This will be cutting it close, but I need to figure out about this prophecy and see if they have a leak within the Coven's inner circle." He pulled out of the parking lot of the bank and headed to my apartment.

Really? Did he really think that he would be going on his own? Boy, he had another think coming. I crossed my arms over my chest and glared daggers at him. I would not be left behind.

"Well, sir, you better call the airline and book another ticket because I'm coming with you." I pushed all of my, *I will not be cowed by you* look at him, but he did not seem impressed. And that pissed me off. I was not some delicate little flower who needed to be sheltered. I could not just sit back and hide. I have been running and hiding my whole damned life. It's time I pulled up my big-girl panties and started acting like a grown-ass witch. I straightened my spine, ready for this fight.

"Delaney, you have to stay here. If the Coven finds out about you, there's no way they would let you leave." His tone said he was ready for this fight too.

I narrowed my eyes at him. "So, you would have me hide like a coward?"

"No, I would have you hide like an intelligent person. The Coven isn't a joke. They will use you, then likely kill you."

"Reid, really, I can handle myself. I'm going with you." If this male thought he was going to control me, boy he had another think coming. Reid's jaw was clenched and he had a white-knuckled grip on the steering wheel. He didn't say another word until we walked into the apartment. For a few seconds I thought I'd won.

Reid shut the door behind him. I could feel the tension radiating off him in waves. I didn't understand why he was so angry at me. I just wanted to be there when we figured all of this out.

"Delaney, listen to me. I need you to stay here. You know what the Coven would do if they knew about you. Mil knew this, that's why she hid you for so long." His tone was the same one used when dealing with a petulant child. Really? We were going to go with low blows?

"Reid, listen to me. I need to go. I don't give two shits about the Coven." I really didn't care; they could chase me all they wanted. "So, what? I stay here and do what? Wait to be attacked?" I was spitting the words at him. Hell, I was pissed.

"No, Mitch will be here to help you with things with Mil. He will be here to..."

"Babysit me," I finished. I rolled my eyes at him. I was so over this whole debacle. I wanted to click my heels together three times and maybe my life would be normal again. *There's no place like normal, there's no place like normal, there's no place like normal.*

"Damnit! Please just let me handle this." He walked over to the kitchen counter and turned his back to me, placing his hands on the linoleum. He was clearly getting mad. Good, now he knew how I felt.

"Fine, you want me to stay with Mitch? Done. Maybe he and I can go out to dinner." It was dirty and it wasn't fair. I wanted to stuff the words back into my mouth as soon as they left. There was an audible snap. I was willing to bet it was the sound of my counter breaking. *Great, my security deposit so would not cover that.* "Reid, I…"

He held up his hand, still not facing me. It was a gesture of hold the hell on. I shut my mouth with a click. It may have been low of him to mention Mil right now, but what I said went beyond low. I played on his fear and jealousy. *Shit. I really do know how to fuck shit up.* He turned around to face me. He only had an amused look on his face.

"Delaney, you do what you like. If that means going out with Mitch, then by all means, have at it." He crossed his arms over his chest. He looked so cold and detached. His words stung like little fire ants over the whole of my body.

"Reid, I'm sorry. I didn't mean that." What else could I say? I wanted what we were; I didn't want him to be so cold.

"Delaney, it's fine. We have no commitment here. You are free to do what you want, just as I am." Again his voice sent a chill through my body.

"Reid, is that how you really feel? Me putting a foot in my mouth aside, is that what you want?" I knew in my bones I was born to love this man. But, that meant nothing if he couldn't return it.

His lips formed a white line and his caramel eyes were flaked with green. He was so hard to read and my heart began to beat ever faster with each moment that passed. Finally, I knew he made up his mind when his face grew colder.

"Yes, Delaney." He turned to go. My head, my heart, hell my whole body ached to stop him and slap some sense into him. My heart was irrevocably broken. His actions put the spike in my heart and his words were the hammer to shatter it. I knew he loved me, but he didn't know it yet. I would not make him stay even though that went against what every cell in my body was yelling. When he reached for the knob of the door it took everything in me not to run at him.

"Bye, Delaney," he said, opening the door.

I said nothing in return. When he shut the door to my apartment, I half wondered if that door was more than a physical barrier; I wondered if he was shutting himself on the other side not just to leave, but to shut himself off from me. I hated that fucking door.

REID JAMISON
FIFTEEN

WE HAD LITTLE MORE THAN FOUR DAYS BEFORE whoever was hunting Delaney would surely try again. I was due to arrive in Dallas in about an hour and I could not get her out of my head. I had made a royal mess of things, and done something I'd never done before. I left. I walked out of her door and didn't look back. *What the hell is wrong with me?* She had said something that was out of line and I pushed her away. Why? Hell, well duh, because I refused to open my heart to anyone since Beth. So, knowing Delaney was falling in love with me, I saw an opening to get out and, like an asshole, I took it.

I put my head into my hands and rubbed my temples. Now, because I was a coward, she was back in Savannah with Mitch. The thought of him and her had a low growl starting in my throat. The thirty-something man sitting next to me shifted a fraction of an inch away. I didn't blame him, as I was in the foulest of moods.

About an hour later, I landed at the Dallas/Fort Worth International Airport. I only packed a small carryon bag as I could not afford to stay here long. I had to figure this out and only had four days to do it. I knew the Coven was the key to this whole thing. Now, I just had to get a group of uptight bureaucrats who never open up to outsiders, to talk to me about their most closely guarded secret that I somehow stumbled across. Yeah, I bet they wouldn't ask questions and they would be ready and willing to talk to me.

Bottom line, I had to protect Delaney. She was powerful, probably more so than she or I even knew, but if the whole of the inner circle of the Coven was after her, I'm not sure even I would be enough to keep them from getting to her.

When I called the Coven to set up this meeting, I had to stretch the truth slightly. Hell, more like I had to strap the truth to me then bungee-jump off the Eiffel Tower with it. I told them we had a lead, but I was made aware that they may be in danger and needed to speak with the inner circle as soon as possible. These assholes were so arrogant they got me on the fastest flight out here. Above all else, the Coven wanted to protect their own asses. Once these killings got the attention of the media and the human government, that was when the damned Coven had called. Not when the first witch, registered or not, lost her life.

I walked out of two sliding doors to find a black town

car waiting by the curb. Outside of the car stood an elderly man who reminded me of a raisin; he had so many wrinkles and folds on his loose skin. In his hands he held a sign that read, *Reid Jamison*. I walked over to him and felt his power before I even touched him. I offered my hand to shake his. He looked at my hand and then looked at me.

"I'm Reid, nice to meet you." I left my hand, trying desperately to be nice.

The old man looked me over then said, "ID."

I dropped my hand and pulled out my wallet, slipped out my license then handed it to the man. He looked it over with brisk practicality, then reached in his pocket and pulled out a clicker to the car. With the press of a button, the trunk popped open.

"Put your stuff in the trunk. Then get in the car, wolf." He spat the word *wolf* as if it were simply distasteful to even say.

"I'll hold my stuff, thank you." He handed me my license back and then slipped into the driver's seat. *Well, wasn't he just the picture of hospitality.* I shut the trunk and got in the passenger seat. I hated riding shotgun, but it was better than the back and I was afraid I would give the guy a heart attack if I drove. He started the car, giving me very little time to fasten my belt.

The Coven was based in Dallas, Texas. There was a large reservation just north of Dallas, near Plano, and that was where the inner circle of the Coven had their headquarters.

I had been here once before with Mitch, when the Coven first asked us to investigate these murders. I should have known they didn't give us all of the information. But, I had to see them. I just knew they were the key to keeping Delaney safe. After what I said, would she even want me? *Do I want her to want me? Shit, I don't know what I want anymore.*

It took about thirty minutes to get to the reservation. Once we got through security, we arrived at the main building. The building was a somewhat small, white-brick, rectangular structure. On the surface, one would think it had only three stories. But, the reality is the headquarters had a vast network of underground levels. The inner circle of the Coven met in one of the lower levels.

As much as the Coven wanted people to be afraid of them, I was not swayed into fear. Witches and weres could always recognize each other. There was a strange feeling of otherworldly power, almost as though we were separates of a whole. After what Delaney told me, about where we both originated from, that seemed to be the case.

Every witch we passed in the hallway to the elevator looked at me with disgust. *What a friendly bunch they are.* Then it all made sense. I almost laughed at what was so obvious. They hated me not just for being a were, but from the bullshit the inner circle was spouting. I bet these people had no idea why they hated me. But, the inner circle knew. I was a reminder of the power they lost and was a threat to the power they had retained. It's amazing what knowing that prophecy could illuminate.

"Here is the key. Go to the tenth sublevel. This is a private meeting so I cannot escort you down there." The driver's tone indicated that he was happy about not having to go any farther with me. *Prick.*

I held out my hand for the key and gave him my best predatory smile. "You've been so kind. I'll be sure to send you a thank you note." He placed the key in my hand and turned to walk away. I took a deep breath in through my nose and smiled. The smell of fear was a sweet one and my wolf revealed in it.

I stepped into the elevator. It was paneled in wood and had gold accents. It looked like it was about as outdated as the rest of the building. The decorations were straight out of the 1970s. I quite liked them, as they reminded me of what my time should have been. There was a brass panel on the right side of the door and several buttons, but only one key hole. I slid the key into the slot, then pressed the button for the ninth sublevel. Dumbass upstairs must have thought I was stupid or he just wanted to be a dick when he told me the tenth. One, I had been here before, and two, witches did everything in groups of nine when possible. It's a magical number to them. Although there were twelve sublevels and three main levels, there would only be one place for the Coven to meet.

There were nine members of the inner circle. Two witches from each element and then an overall leader of the Coven. The leader of the Coven was said to be the most powerful witch. They served a lifetime term. Once they died, the others searched for a new Coven leader, most likely a member of the inner circle already. Seemed like a breeding ground for corruption to me. But, who was I to judge? Werewolves were fairly organized within a pack. But, we tended to be too dominant to be ruled by one being. When a bunch of weres who are not pack get together, our natures tended to take over and it can become mass chaos.

Mitch always said we would never progress unless we were organized and public. He had been the biggest supporter among the alphas across the States, but was met with a lot of resistance, from both the weres and the Coven. Mitch even tried to recruit me, but I preferred to stay out of pack issues. I just did my job and hunted down cheating spouses, found missing people, and used my skills to help solve murders like these. Now, if I could clear Delaney out of my head long enough, I might be able to figure this whole thing out.

The elevator came to a slow stop and the doors opened to a short hallway that led to a metal double door. The walls were all chiseled stone. I was told that because the inner circle could no longer meet in a stone circle outside, they liked to be surrounded with as much nature as possible. Hence, why the main room was nothing but stone walls and ceiling, and a dirt floor.

I opened the larger metal door and the scent of damp

earth assaulted my nose. I had to shake my head from how strong it was. It took my eyes a moment to adjust to the dim lighting. The room was about forty feet in diameter, and while it was in a type of old-world surrounding, it was anything but. The inner circle had power and this stone room showed it.

There were nine large white and gold marble pillars encircling the room. In the middle stood an impossibly large black table. It was at least twenty feet in diameter. The table itself was a mystery. It was most certainly made of the darkest obsidian I had ever seen. It was, amazingly, all one piece that had certainly been chiseled by hand. I could only imagine it had been pulled whole from the bowels of the earth and didn't care to think of the power required to achieve it.

As I walked into the room, the members of the inner circle were already sitting around the table. On my direct left sat the two representatives from Air, Genevieve Terence and Helen Davis. Both women had a power level of eight. Next to them were the representatives of Fire, Jerome Withers and Jayne Milton. Again, both were at an eight, power-level wise. In the middle sat the Coven leader, a Fire witch named Bernard Tailor. His power level was a ten. To his left sat the representatives from the Water witches, Erin Franks and Herald Pitman. Erin at a nine and Herald an eight. Last, to my right sat the representatives from Earth, Monique Thomas and Sylvia Stern. Both were nines. Theoretically, these were the most powerful witches in the States, and arguably the world. I looked at each one, and even though the power in the room was so thick I could practically reach out and touch it, it did not feel anything like the power Delaney had. As if I didn't already know, this only solidified that fact that they could never know or get their hands on her.

I walked up to the empty chair pulled it out and sat down like I owned the place. The glares staring back at me held a lot of questions. But, unlike the driver, there was no fear in this room.

"Reid Jamison. You asked to meet with us to discuss a breakthrough. Please let us know so we may issue our own justice," said the Coven leader, Bernard.

"Well, how about you tell me of the prophecy," I replied, crossing my arms over my chest.

Every single pair of eyes flew to Bernard. And every single gaze was filled with shock and disbelief. *Yeah, that's right, you pretentious assholes. I know.*

"Look, before you can lie and say you have no idea what I'm talking about, save it. Your inability to disclose all of the information has gotten no less than six of these women killed. You knew why this was happening when you hired me. You choose to keep me in the dark and now I have these women's blood on my hands." I was pissed. I hadn't realized how pissed off I was until I was yelling at these self-righteous pricks. And by God if they got Delaney killed, I didn't think I would be able to contain myself.

"Reid," Bernard started. But I would have none of it.

"Mr. Jamison," I countered, "you and your Coven have treated me like an animal from moment one. I put up with it because I wanted to save the witches who were being killed. I don't care about the prophecy; I care about the six witches and their friends and family who have been devastated by your inaction. Now, you tell me who the animal is?"

I made sure to look at each one of them in the eyes as I spoke. They needed to know how their actions affected this case. Clearly, they had never looked at this from another angle. They honestly thought not telling me wouldn't matter. I could see in their eyes that, until this moment, they felt no guilt.

"Mr. Jamison, I think I speak for the whole inner circle when I say that our actions were ill thought out. We sincerely regret not telling you about the prophecy. How can we assist you further?" Bernard's face looked guilt stricken, but his eyes did not mirror what was plastered across his face. He was lying about something, I just didn't know what.

"I already know the prophecy, that explains the hostility toward me, but do you keep a written copy of it? How many people know about the prophecy?"

"Only the inner circle know about it. We hold our positions in the circle until death or we leave voluntarily, but the latter rarely happens. And yes, we have one written copy of the prophecy. It's over a thousand years old so it is kept in a safe and hospitable location," Bernard explained. He was pulling at the French cuffs of his shirt through his Armani suit coat. This man was dressed to the nines. Clearly to impress and intimidate. My wolf was neither impressed nor intimidated. However, my wolf did wonder if he could rip out his jugular without getting blood on the pretty suit.

"Who knows where it is kept? And who has access to it?" They were not going to like what I was about to say.

"Again, only the inner circle knows where it is kept and has access to it."

I said nothing but met each one of their eyes. I was looking for something, some show of guilt. Some show that they knew something more than they did. I saw nothing. Either they were all good actors, which I highly doubted, or they did not know how the information got out.

"Well, the logic says there is a leak." There were soft murmurs around the table. I heard several denials and how this whole thing was outrageous.

"We have nothing to hide at this point. Tell us what you need and we will give it to you. Registered or not, we cannot afford to lose any more sisters." This time it was the lightly Creole voice of Monique Thomas. She genuinely appeared to care and seemed to be the most affected about everything I said.

"I am assuming you have the area where the prophecy is being held under surveillance? I want everything for the year before the first killing. I also will need a room to stay, as I want to be able to be here. We have four days until the next full moon. We have little time to waste," I said, meeting

Monique's dark eyes.

She nodded and said, "Done. You haven't found her, have you?"

I knew the "her" she meant. I looked at her and pushed every bit of resolve in the word I said next: "No."

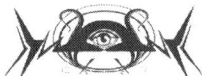

THE INNER CIRCLE STUCK ME IN THE SMALLEST ROOM possible. The bed was a twin size and my feet hung off about eight inches. I think they did it just to make me suffer. *Let's stuff the big guy in a closet with a tiny-ass bed and laugh at him.* I had a stack of twenty-four DVDs to sift through. It would take me forever to find something, but I knew I would. I honestly had no other option but to find something.

Two days I spent cooped up in that tiny room and found nothing. The year before the killing, there had only been a handful of inner circle members who went by to look at the damned case the prophecy was kept in, but none took it out. I had forty-eight hours until the full moon rose and was no closer to finding this guy. I had three disks left to look at and there had to be something there.

I left my small room on the second sublevel in desperate need of caffeine. I walked down the hallway scenting the air for some hint of ... Ah, there it was, just down the hall two doors down on the right. I found a stack of paper cups next to the freshly brewed liquid and poured myself a cup. The scent of Earth grew stronger and was mixed with lavender.

"Hello, Monique," I said just as she rounded the corner.

"How did, ah yes, werewolf," she said, smiling. It was a genuine smile that pinched her eyes at the corners. Monique was tall for a woman. She stood over five feet ten inches and was the type of woman who wore heels on top of her height. She was thirty-two according to her profile and was relatively new to the circle. She had beautiful, rich brown skin and impossibly large dark eyes. Her hair was pulled back in a bun, showing her slender neck.

"So how is the search going?" Her accent was tinged with a bit of that Creole I'd heard in Louisiana.

"Nothing yet. I will find something, I know it," I said, sipping my coffee.

"I hope so. I hate to see any more of our sisters dead. I wanted to tell you from the beginning. I was the new girl and was out voted." This did not surprise me. Monique seemed sweet, but also seemed as though she had a mind of her own and formed her own opinions based on experience, not hearsay. I poured her a cup of coffee and handed it to her.

"You found her, didn't you?" She had lowered her voice to a mere whisper.

The words hung in the air as if they were caught in a spider's web. My eyes flew to hers. *Shit.* She gave me a weak smile. *Do the others know? Fuck me!*

"The others don't know. I just know the way you looked when I asked."

"How did I look?" I couldn't hide now, damnit.

"Like a male wolf protecting his female," she said, still in that low whisper.

"What now? Are you going to tell the rest?" I was a steel rod on the outside, but on the inside I was shaking. *They cannot find out about Delaney*. I clenched and unclenched my fists, trying desperately to get my rage under control. It was way too close to the full moon to lose it.

"I was in love with a wolf once. About two years ago. He broke my heart." She looked down at her hands for a heartbeat. Meeting my eyes, she asked, "Do you love her?"

Without hesitation I said, "Yes." I hadn't even thought about the word until it left my lips. I did love her and I would do anything to keep her safe. Now, I just had to make it back to her and pull my head out of my ass and tell her.

"I won't tell. Just don't break her heart." She looked like she was fighting tears. I hated to see a woman upset.

"I'm sorry he hurt you." What else could I say? This woman held all the cards. She was the outlier that could make or break the future I had with Delaney. *I'm such a moron. All I could say was I was sorry?*

"You're sweet. It's in the past. He did have stunning eyes and rich black hair. His hair reminded me of burnt wood. But, I digress."

Beautiful eyes and black hair. I stood there with the coffee cup an inch away from my lips. I replayed the last thing she said for a good two minutes. Why did it bother me?

Why did this description hit me? Delaney said when she spoke to Sierra, Sierra said the guy she met had…

My eyes flew to hers. "Monique, what was his name?" I tried to curb my excitement. She had unbeknownst to her given me a clue.

"Uh, Michael Smith. Why?" Her tone was weary. I had to calm down. The last thing I needed was a hysterical woman.

Who the hell was that? Had to be a fake name. Or some player I didn't know. Well, that would make sense, considering I didn't know who this ass was.

"When did you break up?" Please say January or February, two years ago. Those were the months I had left to review.

She looked frantic. I put my hands on her upper arms to calm her down.

"Um, January, a few years ago." She was shaking. "Please tell me what's going on."

"Did you tell him anything about the prophecy? I mean, anything at all?" I did everything in my power not to shake her.

She closed her eyes. I was sure she was playing back almost every conversation she could remember having with him. She stood there for a good ten minutes just squeezing her eyes shut. I was going to explode.

"No. I told him about our history. That we split from the Druids. He seemed to know that though. I never said anything about it, though him knowing that was strange." She seemed to sag in defeat or relief. Then suddenly her eyes met mine in horror. "Oh my God. He could have overheard me on the phone with Bernard. This was three months before our split. But, he never said anything. I had forgotten about it."

There it was.

"What did you say on the phone? Do you remember?"

I moved her to a metal chair sitting at a table. I took her coffee from her shaking hand and placed it on the table.

Tears were streaming down her face. I moved a chair and sat down facing her. Her head was in her hands and she was sobbing. I put my hand on her knee and she flinched at my touch. Maybe touching her now was a bad idea.

"I-I-I didn't say much." She took in a breath and blew it out. She did this six or seven times before continuing. "There was a Coven member about twenty some years ago who left the inner circle. She gave no notice, nothing. Then she disappeared. Bernard insisted she was hiding a child. And that we needed to dedicate more resources to finding her. I told him the prophecy could be wrong. That the wolves didn't even know about it." She sobbed once more and gave a small hiccup. "I hung up after that and Michael was watching TV. With your hearing he could have heard me, couldn't he?" She hung her head in defeat.

"Monique, you did not do this. I think this guy was casing you and the whole inner circle. I need to go look at that video. You're welcome to come along, but I don't have much time. My friend and partner, Mitch, is looking over Delaney, but I have to get back to her."

I got up and all but ran to my closet of a room. Everything in this dank tiny room smelled of Earth and mold. I raced to the small bedside table and sifted through the DVDs until I found the one marked, *Jan 1-15.* My hands we shaking as I put the disc in the laptop. I increased the speed so that each day took about three minutes. *Nothing, dammit.* I grabbed the next DVD that read, *Jan 16-31.* I switched the DVDs and pressed play. Nothing! *How the actual fuck is that possible?* I was so sure there would be something here and nothing! I threw the jewel case across the room.

"Look at January eighteenth through the twenty-first again." I looked up to see Monique standing in the doorway. I moved the video bar to the beginning of the eighteenth. I slowed the speed down to where each day was six minutes. Nothing on the eighteenth. Nothing on the nineteenth. My heart rate would have been enough to get a normal man admitted to the hospital. Nothing on the twentieth.

"Wait! Go back to 23:13," Monique said. Her hand rested on my shoulder and she was trembling about as badly as I was. I moved the video bar back to 23:13.

"There!" she shouted. I paused the video. In the still frame was a picture of the gold gilded case the old parchment was encased in. The case seemed to stand about three-and-a-half feet tall, but it was hard to tell from this video.

There was nothing around the case. Wait. I leaned in closer, trying to make out a fly sitting happily on the case. I slowed the video down and zoomed in on the insect. The fly disappeared. I don't mean it flew away; I mean the damned bug was there one second gone the next. *Shit.*

"Someone looped this video," I said, closing the laptop. "How did you know to have me look at those days?" I was sweating. My heart rate was only increasing with every moment that passed.

"Michael broke up with me on the twenty-first. I had a feeling if it were him, that it had to be sometime before then. I did this. I caused all of those deaths," she said, sitting on the bed.

"Listen, this is not your fault, but we don't have much time. Do you have any photos? Anything of his?" *Please say yes.*

"No, I got rid of everything."

Shit, I just needed something, so … new idea. Could he have touched the glass? Fingerprints? That was possible, but I doubted it. Something, anything. I sat there trying to think of something. *Holy fucking shit.*

"You want to help, say, one person?"

She nodded.

"When was the last time that case was opened?" It was getting difficult to hear with the boom-boom, boom-boom thundering in my ears.

"It is only opened when a new inner circle member

comes into the fold."

"I would put money down that says he bypassed whatever alert you have on that case and opened it. It's airtight, correct?"

"Yes."

I gave her a smile with all teeth. "Good. Get me down there and open it."

I got up and walked to the door. This was such a gamble, but I had nothing else.

"Wait, I can't. I mean, I have to call the inner circle. And there is no way they would let you touch it." Her voice was frantic, but honestly I didn't care. I didn't have time for politics.

"Look, I don't want to touch it. I want to smell it." I walked out the door to the elevator and pressed the down arrow. The doors slid open and I stepped in, hearing Monique's footsteps behind me.

"Smell it? Why?" She was slightly out of breath.

"The better to smell him with, my dear." It was the only thing I could think of. This guy had somehow masked his scent from Mitch and me this whole time, but I doubted he would have thought to do so with this.

Monique called several people and had several heated arguments. I really didn't care. I would put my fist through that glass and rip the prophecy to shreds if I had to. In the end, Monique got the okay from Bernard, who was on his way. He told her I was not allowed to touch it. I could not give two shits about what that man wanted.

The prophecy was kept on the tenth sublevel. There was a maze of hallways we had to navigate, with, actually, very few security points. Finally, we stood in front of the gold case. It was the only thing in the white room. The gold fili-gree reminded me of small oak leaves, with thin gold vines that snaked around the glass. There were emeralds, rubies, sapphires, and yellow topaz sprinkled within the leaves and vines on the case. Monique moved to open the case, but I held up a hand.

"Wait." I closed my eyes and inhaled in the scents in the room. I tried to catalog every scent I could. There weren't many, so that helped. I opened my eyes and met her gaze, then nodded. Monique placed the delicately small key in the slot on the top of the case. Slowly, what seemed like forever, she turned the key until I heard a snick of the lock releasing.

"I'll lift the lid and smell around a bit," I said, getting a small smile in return. Monique stepped back and I replaced her position.

I ducked my head and lift the lid up. I inhaled deeply. There was no need to sift through scents. There was no need to catalog each one as it hit me. There was indeed a scent there. I was correct. There was the musk of a werewolf. One I knew very well. That scent hit me like a punch in the gut.

I knew who it was. It belonged to a man I called friend, a man I have known for years. But, it explained so much.

I closed the lid and looked at Monique.

"Well?"

I snarled, then turned and ran down the hallway. I had to get back to Savannah. Back to Delaney. She had no idea the danger she was in. But, I did.

It was him.

DELANEY HAGEN

SIXTEEN

"**M**ITCH. OH, HEY, WHAT'S UP?" I SAID, OPENING the door to my apartment. I really did not want to see anyone.

Today was the day before the full moon and to say I was edgy was putting it lightly. I peeked behind him to see the last burst of orange of the setting Savannah sun. Today we, and by we, I mean me, Troy, and Mitch, held Mil's Requiem and I was still a mess. I tried desperately to push the misery I was in aside. Thank God word did not get to the Coven so I didn't have to contend with them.

"Hey, I tried calling but it went right to voicemail." He seemed annoyed. *Yeah, well, you and me both, buddy.* I may or may not have let my cell phone die two days ago. I just didn't want to talk to Reid or really anyone. And now standing at my doorstep was Mitch. Another macho male. Or as I call him, macho babysitter.

Rubbing my neck I said, "Yeah, sorry, it died and I haven't charged it." I mean, there's no reason to tell him I did it intentionally.

"Avoiding Reid?" he asked, leaning into the doorway. I moved aside and waved him in.

"Not really. Just avoiding everyone." I was such a crappy liar. I could even hear the lie in my tone.

Mitch walked into my kitchen. He turned around in a slow circle, seeming to evaluate my dinky little apartment. Yeah, well, it wasn't much, but it wasn't far from downtown and it's what I could afford.

"Well, senior babysitter, what's up?" I knew me calling him a babysitter pissed him off. But you know what, I was pissed off my opinion didn't matter. I didn't need a babysitter. Maybe I was pissy, but damnit it had been a long month.

Mitch turned to face me. His green eyes sparkled. He really did have amazingly beautiful green eyes. They reminded me a bit of a field of clover. His hands rested on the tops of my shoulders.

"I don't know what's going on with Reid, but I do know you have been through enough this past month for an army of witches. I want to take you out. I know you need to get out of this cell of an apartment. I'm not dumb enough to think you'll have fun, but I want to take your mind off of everything."

Oh lord, please no. I did not want to leave my little bubble. I wanted to stay right here and sulk. I wasn't pouting, though. Okay, maybe I was pouting, but dammit didn't I deserve to pout a little? Wait, was he asking me out on a date? No. Maybe? I was panicking; I could feel it.

"Look, Mitch, I'm flattered but…"

"Whoa, it would not be a date. I would never do that to Reid. No matter how stupid he is."

There was sincerity in his voice. Reid told me he didn't have many friends within the community of weres. He was a lone wolf and that causes issues with many others. But, Mitch was more or less his best friend. I believed him when he said he would never do something like that to Reid. His gaze told me there was no saying no. I sighed and caved. It might be nice to just not have to worry for a bit.

"Okay, let me change and we can go."

He smiled and crossed his arms over his chest, looking so proud of himself. There was a flash of something harsh that crossed his face. It disappeared as soon as it appeared. *I think I was seeing things.*

I picked out a white summer dress. It was a flowing chiffon-type material with thin straps and a deep, open neckline. The dress hung to about mid-thigh. It was such an angelic dress and I never got to wear it. My skin was not too pale, so the white seemed to stand out next to it. I grabbed my white strappy sandals and put them on. I paused. Was this safe? Going out now? It being so close to the full moon. I brushed off the questions. Mitch was here to protect me. He knew what was safe, right?

"Okay, mister nanny, let's go." When Mitch saw me he froze.

He looked me over agonizingly slowly. Had I seen that look on Reid's face it would have set me on fire, but when Mitch did it I had a shiver of ice prick its way up my spine. He looked at me with what could only be described as hunger. I couldn't help but blush. Maybe I should change.

"Wow, Delaney. Reid is an asshole. You look amazing." He licked his bottom lip. He actually licked his lips. *Sheesh.* "Oh, Reid called. He was pissed he couldn't get a hold of you. But, he will be here tomorrow."

"Did he find anything?" Gone were any thoughts of Mitch. I hoped like hell Reid found something.

"I don't know. He wouldn't tell me over the phone. He just said to take care of you." Mitch's voice wavered for the briefest of moments. "Let's go."

I wished Reid was here. Not just because I was irrevocably in love with him, because I was, but because I really didn't know how safe I really was. I looked over at Mitch and shook my head. This was Reid's best friend and he trusted him. I needed to get out of my own head and just go with it.

"Yes, let's," I said, opening the front door.

WE WENT TO CHURCHILL'S PUB FOR DINNER. MITCH MAY have looked like a god, but man he had the personality the so-called benevolent sprit gave a carrot. We chatted about sports. Yeah, not the most exciting thing, but I did find out Mitch loved ice hockey. Bless the man, he didn't even bring up Mil, werewolves, Reid, witches, nothing. It was stupid, mindless conversation and I loved him for it.

"Would you like to go walk along the river and get a drink, then I'll take you home?" he asked as he stood up from the table. He offered me his hand and I stared at it. *Should I?* I mean, I don't drink much, but I liked the fact that my mind wasn't wandering with this not-date outing. I placed my hand in his and stood up from the table.

"Sure." I gave him a shy smile. *Had I met Mitch first, maybe I would feel differently?* Well, if I'm being honest, not much would have changed about the situation. I just didn't have the heat like I did with Reid. In fact, it was right weird, the feelings I got with both weres. Reid was all spark and heat. Mitch felt like nothing but ice. I have never touched someone and felt frozen like I did with Mitch.

River Street wasn't too crowded, as it was a Monday night. There were still a few tourists milling around and young adults shooting in and out of the bars. We walked over to the railing by the river.

"Would you like a drink?" Mitch asked.

"Sure, Amaretto Sour." I went for my purse, but Mitch stopped me with a scowl.

"Don't even think about it. You stay here. I'll be able to see you from the bar. I'll be right back." Before he left he picked up my right hand and placed a gentle kiss along my knuckles. It felt like shards of ice exploding in my hand, just from his touch. I shivered. I think he took that as a good sign. He may have said he wouldn't turn this into a date, but I sure was getting some mixed signals.

I turned around to watch the Savannah River. I always thought Sierra was lucky to be a Water witch. Her element was so beautiful and people would get too distracted by the grace of it and forget just how deadly it really was. Sierra would always say, "I like to think of the elements a witch can control as a beautifully crafted sword. Like any good weapon it needs to be beautifully distracting, but still hold an edge."

"Don't jump." I may not have jumped, but I did start at the sound of Mitch's voice. He handed me my drink and smiled. He really did have beautiful eyes. They seemed to sparkle when he smiled. *Damn him.*

"Sorry, you startled me," I said, taking the drink from him and taking a sip. The sour flavor more than overwhelmed the sweet of the Amaretto. My face squinted with the taste.

"Oh no. Is there something wrong?" he said worriedly.

"No, just a lot of sour. Must be a new guy." I stirred the little straw in an attempt to mix the drink up a bit. I took another sip. Much better. "No worries. Just needed a good stir."

We sipped our drinks and sat in silence watching the water. The lights reflecting off the surface looked like little dolphins jumping in and out of the still water. After about ten minutes those lights began to swirl. I looked down at my drink and realized I finished it. *Man, I know I don't drink, but that must have been stronger than I thought.* I stood up and, well, didn't quite make it all the way up. I wisely decided to stay seated. *Man, that drink is hitting me hard.* When did fog roll in? *Shit.* Why was it so damned foggy? I shook my head to try to clear it, but with little success. I looked over to where Mitch was sitting.

"Hey, Mitch." My words were slurring. "Could you grab me a water?" He looked over at me and smiled. He looked like a kid on Christmas morning.

"Sure I can. Are you feeling okay?"

"Yeah, that drink hit me pretty hard. I'm not much of a drinker," I said, trying to stand up. I was a little wobbly and unsteady, but I did manage to get my feet under me. Mitch rushed over to me and grabbed my elbow.

"Hey, let's get you home." His voice sounded distant. It sounded like he was talking through a long metal tube.

I nodded. I couldn't really remember what I was nodding at, but we started walking. We walked over the uneven cobblestone for what felt like six hours. I fell at least six times. After what felt like a week of walking, we got to Mitch's car.

"Mitch, should I be feeling like this after one drink?" Had I said that? Could I still speak? God, the world was spinning.

Mitch looked at me with an annoyed expression. "Just sit back and close your eyes."

I knew deep down I shouldn't close my eyes. I knew something wasn't right. But, for the life of me, I couldn't figure it out. Something happened. I forced my eyes open. The car was moving at supersonic speed. *What is this called? Ludicrous speed. The world is going plaid. Is that even possible outside of Spaceballs?* God, even my thoughts were rambling. Soon my eyes were coated in lead and keeping them open was an act in futility. Just before my eyes fluttered shut I saw my street wiz by.

"Wait, you missed…"

"Shhh. Delaney, it's okay," a voice said. I knew it wasn't okay. My soul was beating at the inside of my body, but there was nothing I could do. The world narrowed to a single point, a single flame, then went out.

REID JAMISON
SEVENTEEN

D UE TO INCLEMENT WEATHER, IT TOOK ME NEARLY a day just to get back to Savannah. Tonight was the full moon and I had to find Delaney. I tried calling her no less than three thousand times, but every time it went to her voicemail. Of course I tried to call Mitch, but he didn't answer. No shocker there, considering he's the one who's been killing all of these witches. I punched the steering wheel in frustration.

No wonder I couldn't smell anyone on the bodies or at the scenes, the fucking killer had been there the whole time. His smell was all over everything. I didn't think twice about his scent being on the victims or anywhere because he was with me. I was so stupid. I couldn't see past our friendship. And now Delaney was caught up in my stupidity. I had to find her.

I raced through Savannah, through traffic and tight

turns. I broke no less than thirty traffic laws. It only took me thirty minutes to get from the airport to Delaney's parking lot. I parked the car and ran up to her door.

As I got close to her door I saw a piece of paper taped to the wood, flapping in the slight breeze. I could smell Mitch from here. Cold washed over my body and made my hackles rise. I took a second to look around and survey. Nothing seemed out of the ordinary. I returned my attention to the flapping note. I tore it free of the tape and opened it.

Reid,

I'm sure by now you know who I am. I am also sure you know who I have. She sure is pretty. Who knows the things I will do to her. I will send you a text message at 7 p.m. Go to the address I provide and maybe there will be some scraps left for you.
Mitch

I crumpled the paper in my hand. I would kill him. I would rip him apart. This couldn't just be him though. He had to have involved his whole pack. There was no way that Mitch had to skills to pull off some of the shit that has gone down. Looping a video feed? Breaking into the inner circle's building in the middle of a reservation? No way. But the act of killing these women, that was all Mitch. So, this was a trap then? I had no choice but to go and risk it. How had he gotten Delaney? He had to have subdued her because she would never have gone willingly. *Shit!* Why hadn't she had her phone on?

I sat down with my back resting on Delaney's door. What else could I do at this point? I had a fight coming and I needed to prepare myself for it. There would be only one way to fight Mitch if his pack was truly involved: I had to challenge him as alpha.

I could call other wolves. I did have a few hours. But, who would I call? I had spent my whole life as a werewolf shunning others and isolating myself. I had no other friends to call. I had no one that would aid me. And Mitch knew it.

I had so many questions. Why? What was the point of this? I banged my head against the door. Maybe that would settle the wolf a bit. I closed my eyes and pictured the wolf I'd called friend and partner. I never trusted him 100%. I should have questioned that, but I didn't trust anyone. Except for Delaney. I would get her out of this, I would save her, even if that meant ripping that entire pack apart.

I pushed all thoughts away and focused on blanking my mind. I had to keep my thoughts clear. I wanted nothing in my way.

My phone jolted me out of my meditation. It was a text from Mitch. I got up and walked to the car. He gave me such a narrow window there would be next to no time to get to Delaney. I put the address in to my GPS and it was just as I thought. It was about an hour southwest of Savannah and I was only given until 8:10 P.M. to get there. I got in the car and turned the engine over. I was going to kill him. There would be no doubt about it.

It only took me about fifty minutes to get to the location. The sun was almost set and it cast a dark, purple hue on everything. I drove down along a dirt road and honestly thought there would be just an empty lot. But, once the dust settled down, I was able to see a small building about a quarter of a mile in front of me. As soon as the building was visible I parked the car and got out and paused to scent the air. The smell of dirt and dry brush seemed to mask several of the underlying scents. I got Mitch's scent. I caught scents of a number of other weres. I took a deeper breath and that's when I caught the slight scent of gardenias. It was Delaney. The wolf inside me riled and began to fight for control. *Calm down. Soon.*

With all of the other wolves here, I would have no choice but to challenge him. Now the real question would be, could I beat him? He and I had never fought, as we were both a little too dominant for that, but I have seen him fight and he was particularly ruthless. I have fought my fair share, but had hoped to never have to fight Mitch.

As I walked, the building came into view. It looked to be a long building made of red brick, a forgotten police station. The mortar between the bricks had all been eaten away from the ivy and moss growing on it. Half the building was covered in the green parasites. Speaking of parasites, Mitch stood outside in front of the entrance.

"Reid, I see you made it," Mitch called. His voice filled the distance between us, nearly causing me to charge him and rip at him with every bit of the beast inside me.

"Mitch, where is she?" I really did not want to beat around the bush about this. I stopped about fifty feet in front on him. Now, I couldn't see the others from his pack, but I could hear them.

"She's here. Still asleep, I think. We had a big date last night. She wore this tiny little white dress. She looked so good I could have just eaten her up." He smiled through each word.

I choose to ignore the fact he was trying to play my emotions.

"Why are you doing this? Because you think some prophecy is going to come true? How deluded can you be?"

"I AM NOT DELUDED!" His voice thundered over the grass and reverberated off the walls of the building. "The Coven has been hiding our true origins and this prophecy for a long time. It is time to take them out of the equation. The prophecy is real. Just think of the power we will have once she's changed! A wolf with a witch's power?" Holy shit, he really believed this could happen.

"It is impossible to change a witch! Look at the witches you have already killed!" He was out of his mind.

"They were necessary losses. They led me to the one witch who could survive the change."

"I challenge you for rule of your pack." I was done talking to this man. I was incensed; I needed to rip him apart.

His face honestly looked shocked. What did he think, I would come here and lay down my life without a fight? He really had lost his mind if that were the case. Even from here I could see his jaw tighten. This forced him to abide by the rules of a challenge. This took his pack out of the equation.

"Accepted." He turned and stepped in the building.

I knew what he was doing. He was shifting. Anytime a position like alpha was challenged, it must be done in wolf form. I pulled off my shirt and I kicked off my shoes, then I shifted out of pants and boxer-briefs. I closed my eyes and started the shift, setting my humanity aside and pulling the wolf to the forefront. Pain lit across my skin and deep in my bones. The shift only took about three minutes because of the full moon, but it was always incredibly painful shifting that fast. I shook my head and body to try to alleviate some to the long-lasting tingles and aches.

After a shift everything is more vivid. Colors are brighter, shadows aren't as dark, noises are crisp, and scents are more distinguished. That's how I knew I was in more shit than I realized. Because just about every member of Mitch's pack was here. I scented no less than twenty werewolves, not including myself. Rules of challenge state that there should be no interference of fight, or there will be justice dispensed by the alpha. When it was a fight with the alpha, another alpha should be present to act as a reminder to others not to cheat or interfere. There were no such guarantees now. I just had to be smarter than him.

In my wolf form I was a tawny blond color. Mitch, however, was solid black. I was both bigger and taller than Mitch in wolf form, but the bastard was fast as a rat. Mitch stepped out of the doorway with his second in command trailing behind him. His second in command stood about five foot ten inches. His name was Matthew Gingham, and he reminded me of a used car salesman. One look at the guy with his bald head and his craggy face and you would think sleezeball. I told Mitch a number of times he needed to send that guy to another pack. He just oozed disgusting. Guess he and Mitch were cut from the same cloth.

"You have challenged our alpha. He has accepted your challenge. This is not a fight to the death. There will be an option to submit. Just before the killing blow you will have the option to yield. If you do not submit you forfeit your life. Do you agree to these terms?" His voice seemed to boom across the fifty or so feet that separated us. I gave a short howl. Then Mitch followed with a short yip.

Unlike our brother wolves, other pack members are forbidden to interfere with a fight. I, however, did not think anything was out of the realm of possibilities today. I bared my teeth and snarled. I would not tap out of this fight. He would have to kill me.

I made the first move and charged him. So much of a fight between weres was spent controlling our beast and thinking tactically like a human. We were not human. You can dress us up in pretty clothes and put us in a job with the rest of humanity, but when it came down to it, we were not human. I have no need to dance with my beast when it comes to this fight and this form. I set him free.

I was met with snarling teeth and a snapping jaw. We both met standing on our hind legs, reaching for each other's faces with paws. My jaws caught nothing but air and the occasional clump of fur. But, he wasn't landing any blows either. I backed away, turning my back to him. But, just as fast, I turned around and met his charge with my open jaws. I bit down, hard, and heard Mitch yelp. I had the meat at his front right shoulder in between my teeth. I bit even harder, feeling his skin give way and the taste of blood filling my mouth.

The taste ratcheted my thundering heart up a notch. I began to shake my head to cause a greater injury. While I was thrashing I felt Mitch rip at my right ear. I yelped in pain. Just that second of pain caused me to lose the advantage. I backed away, as did Mitch. I couldn't see the blood on him, but I could smell it. Well, all I could smell was blood. I licked my nose, trying to clear it a bit. My ear throbbed with the pain from his bite. I shook my head, trying to gauge the damage. It was minimal. By this point about seventeen of his pack had formed a circle around us.

It was Mitch who charged first this time. I thought he would go for my throat, but he shifted at the last moment and charged my side, sending me sprawling. He was on me before I had time to right myself. He had the full advantage to end it right then. But, he was too slow. Right as he went for my throat I managed to get my right paw in the way. He clamped down on my paw, crushing the bone. Pain exploded in liquid heat from his bite. I used my hind legs to thrash and kick at him. Finally, after what seemed like far too long, my right hind paw connected with his face and my nails dug into his eye. It was a lucky as hell shot. He howled in pain and I didn't waste time.

I scrambled to get up and press my advantage on him, charging past his snapping fangs. Past his flying claws. Past the rage I felt for him. Past the fur. Past the white-hot pain shooting through every bite and puncture. I sank my teeth into his throat and felt a sharp sting in my back, but it was a bee sting compared to the other bite wounds. I clamped down as hard as I could. I felt the rush of his pulse begin to slow under my teeth. I clamped down even harder. I would rip his head clear off. I felt his body began to grow limp. Just as I started shaking my head my skin was set on fire. Frantically, I released Mitch and ran backward. I had to be on fire. I rolled over in the dirt, trying desperately to relieve the burning covering my entire body. My wolf form was slipping. This had never happened before.

I heard the dirt shuffle near my head. I snapped up on all fours. Standing was pure agony, but I had no other choice. Mitch was circling me. His throat was a mangled mess of torn flesh and matted hair. It would heal. I had him, but something happened. My skin felt like it was covered in lava. It still did. *Shit.* My chest felt like it was caving in. I was having a hard time breathing, like I could only breathe through a straw.

I collapsed on my side and could no longer hold my wolf form. I slowly and agonizingly shifted into my human form. My skin and bones felt like an open wound being filled with peroxide. I have never had such a painful shift.

I looked up to see Mitch standing over me in his human form. Had it taken me that long to shift? He was already half dressed. *Why hasn't he killed me?* The world was swirling and tilted. I gasped for air but found little of it. Mitch smiled, all teeth.

"Now, Reid, did you really think you would beat me?" His voice sounded as though he swallowed gravel. He kicked me in the side. I almost didn't even register the attack. It didn't hold a candle to the pain I was in. I opened my mouth to speak, but no words came out.

"Silver nitrate, my dear lone wolf." He kicked me again. This time he kicked what little breath I had out of me. The air went out of me with a whoosh along with blood. *The mother fucker drugged me.* Silver, no wonder I wasn't healing. Having silver in my blood would preclude me from any kind of accelerated healing.

"You'll have to kill me. I do not yield," I managed between gasps of much needed air.

He made a *tisk, tisk, tisk* noise with his mouth. "I'm not going to kill you. I need you." He made a few hand motions and within moments I was lifted to my feet. I couldn't move. The silver nitrate had done just what Mitch wanted. It had effectively shut me down. This would take my body at least twelve hours to burn off. Who knew what would happen to Delaney in that time.

"Only way you could beat me? Shoot me with silver? Pathetic, really," I taunted. He turned and punched me in the face. I went blind in my left eye. I heard and felt a crunching sound as his punch connected. I guess he was healing at normal werewolf speed because his face still looked like hell, but it didn't dampen his blow. *Shit, that hurt.* I swallowed the pain and smiled up at him. "Thought so."

I couldn't walk so two of his pack dragged me into the building. I barely had enough strength to hold my head up to see where I was being taken. Mitch directed them to take me down a flight of stairs.

"Where is she, Mitch?" I spat the words. I hoped they hit him in the face. The stairwell opened up to a hallway lined with several office doors. The place was musty and smelled of mold. But, there was a slight scent of gardenia and it was getting stronger.

"Don't worry, Reid. Your girlfriend is fine." I couldn't see his face, but his voice was laced with venom.

I wasn't sure what good it would do but I said, "You know I claim her, right."

He laughed. "No matter. It would never have mattered. She's mine now."

I didn't know if it was him blowing off my claiming or him saying she was his. But, whatever it was set me off. I found the last bit of energy and turned. I tossed the two assholes aside and charged at Mitch. I must have caught him off-guard because I slammed his worthless body against the wall. My forearm crushed his windpipe. I had no illusion that this was little more than posturing, but I was incensed. I pressed all of my weight into my arm.

"I. Will. Kill. You." I said each word as though it were a curse. I spat each syllable and pushed every bit of my power behind them. Just before I was pulled off of him, he looked scared. *Good.* He should be wetting his pants.

They pulled me to a nearby room. There were chains and shackles fixed to the wall. From the shine of lights bouncing off the shackles, I could tell they were silver. Across from the wall with the chains there was a large window that looked to be a two-way mirror. *Looks like they picked this location with purpose.* They shackled me to the wall. There was little at this point that I could do. I could barely move. Breathing hurt. Fuck, but the pulse in my neck hurt.

"Look, there is your little Delaney," Mitch said coolly.

I looked up to see Delaney through the window. She was shackled as I was. But, her hands were chained to something I couldn't make out. And she was unconscious. I fought my restraints, with little results.

"What do you want? I'll give you anything. Just let her go." I wasn't above begging, not for her.

Mitch met my eyes and laughed. "I want her. And I have her. You'll see the rest."

I looked past Mitch to Delaney strung up on the wall. I loved her. Beyond this world and the next, I loved her. Now, I had to find a way to save her. Or pray she came back to me.

DELANEY HAGEN
EIGHTEEN

"WHERE ARE WE?" I LOOKED AROUND AND everything was hazy.

There was a heavy fog layered on the ground. I couldn't see past my knees. There were pine trees all around me. They were so tall I could only see their trunks. The man next to me looked at me adoringly. I have known him my whole life. He had been in every dream I've had since I was a child. I knew him in a way that felt intimate. But, I didn't know him at all. I knew better to ask for his name. Not just because I knew he wouldn't tell me, but because I wasn't too sure I wanted to know.

"We are where you want us to be." His slight eastern-European accent tickled the hairs on the back of my neck.

Now what the hell does that mean? I bent down to run my fingers through the fog. It swirled around my fingers. Did fog really do that?

"Is this a dream?" I looked up at him and met his near-black eyes.

"Yes."

"I don't understand." I didn't; I had no idea why I was here or why he was here.

"Take us somewhere that means the most to you and I will tell all." He grabbed my hand.

"How, I don't know…" I looked around and the foggy forest was replaced by a familiar campsite. It was the same campsite that Sierra took me to. The first time I got to touch wild lightning. Now, it was dark. Sometime in the middle of the night. It must have been near morning though, because the night sky was purpling around the edges.

"I hoped this would be where you picked." He smiled down at me. His black hair was loose and fell over his shoulders.

"Why am I here?" I questioned.

"Because you are dreaming."

"Okay, why are you here?"

"I have a gift for you, and I need something from you." It was strange, this man. I tried to think back to other dreams he was in and I did not recall him ever speaking to me.

"Care to elaborate?" Good grief, but he was being obtuse.

"It will be hard to understand. But, I will tell you," he said, reaching out his hand to me. I looked down at it as though it were covered in snakes. I wasn't sure I wanted what he offered. But, hell, here I was and it did not seem like I was going anywhere, so I might as well. I placed my hand in his and we walked.

"Well, what can I do for you?" I said, looking at the ground.

He laughed out loud. It was a rich, filling sound. It seemed to touch my soul and fill it some.

"Oh, little one, you never cease to surprise me."

"Well, I just want to know for once what is going on." I was getting frustrated being in the dark.

"I am sorry." He stopped walking and turned me to face him. I met his gaze and fought the fleeting sensation to run the hell away and not look back. "I have something to give you before you wake. I need you to hold on to it until the time is right."

I opened my mouth to ask, but he just smiled, causing me to shut my lips.

"You will know when. As for what I need from you." He put a hand on either side of my face, cradling it. "I want your fear and your pain. I want you to send it to me."

"I don't understand." I wanted to give him everything as long as he kept touching me. This man was dangerous.

"You will be more afraid than you have ever been. When you are, I want you to send me your fear, your panic, and I will send you calm. The pain will seem earth shattering, but release it to me and I will soothe you." He spoke the words fear, panic, and pain as though they were tangible. Like I

261

could pick them up, put them in a box, and wrap Christmas paper around them.

"I'll try," was all I could manage.

"Now, we do not have much time."

He drew me in and crushed his lips to mine. It took me so off-guard all I could do was stand there like a mannequin. After a moment I opened my mouth and felt a rush of life enter my body. Thank God his hands were on my shoulders, otherwise I would have blown away like a feather in the wind. He was breathing life into me. That's the only way to explain it. This was not a kiss that warmed me like I shared with Reid. This was somehow more. He was truly breathing something more into me. He was filling me, expanding me. Just when I thought I would burst he let me go. I staggered backward a few steps before finding my feet again.

"What did you give me?" I could feel it there in the corner of my soul. It was just more. More than me alone.

"Your future." He looked to the sky and frowned. My gaze followed his to the now burnt-orange sky. All that was left in the sky from the night was the large full moon.

"There is little time. One more thing," he bent down slightly to whisper in my ear, "I will take the pain and fear if you let me. Remember, night cannot last forever. The moon will set and the sun will rise. I promise you, no matter how bad it gets, it will get better. I love you, my little lightning bug." He kissed the tip of my nose and faded away.

Calling after him yelling questions wouldn't do a

damned thing. I sat down in the field and waited to wake up and face my future.

I TRIED TO STRETCH BEFORE I OPENED MY EYES. BUT, I couldn't lift my arms. *What the hell is going on?* My body felt like it took a trip in a drying machine. Every part of me hurt and my head was going to explode, I just knew it. I cracked my eyes. Bright light flooded my vision and just as fast I clamped my eyes shut. I should have been more panicked about the fact that I couldn't move more than a few inches, but my mind was too busy trying to catalog and sift through all of the shit I had just been through.

What the hell happened? The last thing I remembered other than that weird-ass dream was having dinner with Mitch. We went and had a drink and then, nothing. My memories were a mess of foggy images. I tried to sift through them, but just could not manage it. Finally, I opened my eyes slowly, letting my eyes adjust to the painful light.

After a few moments I realized that it wasn't that bright. I looked around the small room and it took a good five minutes for the full effect of this situation to register. I was chained to a wall. *CHAINED, who does that?* My hands were taped to two rods on either side of my body. I laughed. Hell, I guffawed. I mean, what else could I do? *I can't even make this shit up.* Granted, I may have been suffering from a bit of hysteria.

"Hello?" My voice was dry so I sounded a bit horse. "Can someone either kill me or get me some water?" I was just so done with this. I heard footsteps outside of the dusty and dirty dank cellar of a room. It looked like it was once some kind office space, but had been forgotten for about fifty years. The doorknob turned and standing in the door-way was Mitch.

"Hello, princess. Did you sleep well?" His tone carried a mocking coldness to it.

The memories of the drink he had gotten me, the weird facial expressions, and the last memory of him passing my apartment all came back to me in a wash of ice water across my mind. I met his eyes and pushed all my hatred at him. Instinctively, I reached for the power in my core and the power flooded me. Then cold reality slapped me in the face. I had no way to expel the lighting. Whatever he taped my hands to had absorbed the lighting that jumped from my body. My heart was beating like a wild thing. Had Reid been in on it too? *Please, no.*

"Where's Reid?" I said.

"He's here." His tone was even. What did that mean? Could he really be part of this? *Shit.*

"Why? Why do any of this?" He moved from the door, shuffling his feet and kicking up dirt and dust. He stopped about three inches from touching me. I could feel his hot breath touching my face like delicate fingers.

"If this prophecy is true, then you, little girl, will be the end of the witches." He raised his hand to my face and ran a finger along my jaw, then down my neck. He fingered the shiny pink skin of the wound on my collarbone.

"I should have been more careful with you. I didn't mean to bite you. But, I wanted to see what was so secretive about your power. And boy did I figure it out." His eyes followed the path his finger was making along my skin. His touch was so cold it left goose flesh in its wake.

"That was you?" His finger dipped down to the swell of my breasts. He met my eyes and his own sparkled. A smile broke out over his face.

"Yes, now tell me. What do you know of the prophecy? What did your aunt tell you?"

I couldn't be sure if it was the word *aunt* that tipped me over the edge or the thought of how many innocent people he killed to get to me. I pushed my power outward. The main way I had to push my power was through my hands, but I have radiated power over the surface of my body before. I focused my power and thought of it like a blanket and covered myself with it. As soon as my power snapped into place, Mitch snatched his hand from me. He looked at me as though he disapproved. *Good*, I hoped I pissed him off. If he thought for one fucking second I would be going gently into that good night he had another think coming!

Just as fast as I had my little victory, it faded as his hand connected with my cheek. He slapped me so hard my teeth bit down on my tongue.

"Tell me," he demanded, rubbing his hand. I spat the blood that was pooling in my mouth at him.

"She told me I was the only witch who could be turned. She said I would be the downfall of the witches. That's all I know." I thought about lying to him, but figured maybe I could get some information from him too if I played ball.

"You know next to nothing about the prophecy," he scoffed. At this point I didn't care.

"Where is Reid?" Had he hurt him? I feared that more than him being in on this whole thing.

"He's here. One thing you need to know about this prophecy is that you will need to let me turn you willingly." He managed to say it with a straight face.

"Yeah," I laughed, "that's so not going to happen."

He smiled and said, "Oh, honey, that's what Reid is here for." He gestured at the wall in front of me. I realized belatedly that it wasn't a wall at all. It was a large window.

It was as though the curtain was raised on a stage. The blackness was gone. If I could have fallen to my knees I would have. My eyes burned with tears. The tears felt like liquid heat carving paths down my cheeks. Reid was bound to the wall much like I was. He was covered in blood, but didn't look hurt. I screamed his name. He raged against his chains, to no avail. I couldn't hear him through the window.

Mitch knelt in front of me, his head even with my pelvis. He angled himself so he was sideways, then looked at Reid and ran his hand up my thigh. My heart raced. I pushed my power out again, but he must not care about the pain of touching me. I thrashed against my chains, but it did little to dissuade him.

I met Reid's gaze. If his eyes could kill, Mitch would have combusted where he knelt. Reid suddenly raged against his confines, but nothing. *What the hell is in those chains?* It had to be supernatural to keep him in them. Mitch's hand stopped right before the apex of my thighs. He smiled up at me.

"I just love pissing him off," he said, standing up. He was rubbing his hand again. I knew it had to hurt; I was pushing hard on my power.

"Hand hurt?" I said, giving him a saccharin sweet smile. When he didn't answer I asked, "How do you plan to use Reid to get me to let you turn me?" As soon as the words left my mouth, I knew. He would kill Reid if I didn't. The realization must have showed on my face because Mitch smiled.

"It's simple, Delaney, I have over ten pack members in the room with Reid. If you fight or hurt me, they kill him. If you accept your fate, I won't kill him."

And there it was. I met Reid's eyes. He knew what Mitch said. He knew through the expression on my face. He shook his head and mouthed, "NO!" I had no doubt that I could agree to this and when he let me out of these restraints I could kill him. But, then Mitch's pack members would most definitely kill Reid. *Shit!* What if the prophecy was real? What if I did come back? God, Mitch better hope I didn't come back because I would kill him. Would he kill Reid anyway? How did he plan to control me if I turned? Shit, I had so many questions.

"What do you think will happen if I do change, Mitch? What do you expect to happen?" I needed to either keep him talking or find out as much as I could.

"Once you turn, and you WILL turn, I will use you to bring down the witches."

"Why do you care about the witches? Why do you want them destroyed so much?"

"When they fall, the weres will rise. We will become public and will infiltrate society," he said with conviction.

"You're deluded."

"ENOUGH! Delaney, do not think for one second I do not have a plan. There is so much more you don't know. It's comical, really." He gestured over to the window.

A man walked over to Reid and pressed a knife to his throat. *Oh God!*

"Wait!" I screamed. Mitch held up a hand to the window. He walked over to me and brushed his thumb down my cheek, trailing the path a tear had made.

Here was the biggest question of all, could I die for Reid? I looked up and met Reid's stony gaze. I loved him. I didn't want to live without him and, frankly, I didn't know that I could. But, did I love him enough to die for him? Did he love me? Did it really matter? I made up my mind when

I crashed into him standing in front of my apartment. *That seems like years ago.*

"I want to talk to Reid." I couldn't even look at Mitch.

"He will be able to hear you, but you will not be able to hear him." Mitch walked over to the window and pressed a button on the wall. "Go."

"Reid?" My voice was so shaky the word seemed to come out in letters only.

He looked up at me.

"I don't know what to do anymore. I don't know what the right answer is." A tear leaked out of my eye. He mouthed the word "NO!" again. Three of Mitch's men came in the door at that moment. One walked over to him and replaced him at the intercom. Mitch began to strip. I knew what he was doing. The other two began unchaining me from the wall. The words of the man in my dream hit me.

"I will take the pain if you let me. Remember, night cannot last forever. The moon will set and the sun will rise. I promise you no matter how bad it gets it will get better. I love you, my little lightning bug."

I closed my eyes as the men tugged and peeled at the restraints. I sent the fear out as though it were a physical object, turning it into a ball just like Sierra taught me long ago, and set it free. My heart slowed and I opened my eyes. The two men undid the last of the shackles. I stood there in my pretty white dress from the night before.

"Reid, I need you to know I love you." My fear was surprisingly gone, but the tears still flowed. It felt like my heart was breaking.

Reid was raging now. He was pulling and thrashing against the chains. I noticed that his cheeks too were lined with tears.

I looked over at the impossibly large black wolf now pacing in front of me. It was him who attacked Troy and me. Not that I doubted it. "You better hope I don't come back. Because if I do, you're dead," I said, glancing over at Mitch, then back at Reid.

"I will love you in this life and the next." I was glad I couldn't hear Reid's protests and screaming. Then he mouthed the one thing that I knew would make this even harder.

"I love you."

"This life to the next, Reid, remember that." My heart lay on the floor with the dust and dirt. It lay there in pieces. They lay there throbbing and trying to beat, but I knew it would never beat again. Not without Reid. That's why I had no choice. I looked at Mitch.

"I give myself freely to Reid, never to you."

Mitch snarled. But, I knew that was all he needed. I didn't know how I knew, but I did. No matter the path I took I would have ended up here. I would have given myself to this fate or any other for him.

I didn't see it coming because I wanted my last sight to be of Reid. His rich caramel eyes, the feel of his touch on my skin, and his soft kisses. Mitch's teeth sank into my neck. There was a rush of pain. But, I did exactly what I was told and balled the pain up and sent it away. I sent the ball of pain hurtling away from my body. I felt my throat ripping with every tug and pull of his jaws. My chest and front grew warm with my life's blood, but little to no pain.

I collapsed to the floor, staring up at the mold-covered ceiling. I grasped at threads, trying to see him one more time, but they were slipping through my fingers, much like the fog in my dream. I felt the world shrink to a single pinpoint. That pinpoint throbbed with the beat of my heart. It expanded and contracted.

I thought of Reid and let go of the last thread.

MITCH SALDANA
EPILOGUE

*I*T'S HER. IT HAS TO BE HER. IF NOT I AM SO SCREWED. I was positive Reid told the son-of-a-bitch Coven it was me. So, time was not on my side. This had to work. I had a meeting with all of the alphas in the country in a matter of two weeks. This would be my only chance to show them our new weapon against the heavy fist of the Coven. The last thing I needed was some pretentious witches knocking down my door. I put all my eggs in this basket and now I hoped it held.

I walked over to the extra bedroom in my Atlanta apartment. Delaney lay on the bed. Killing her had been easy, much like it had been with all the others. This was the only chance I had to have a weapon to use against the Coven. The Coven had long been the driving force stopping the weres from organizing and taking control of the supernatural world, and in time the government. My phone buzzed in my pocket.

"Saldana."

"Alpha, did she wake?" Mark's tinny voice questioned.

I looked over at the dead witch lying on the bed. It was the height of the new moon tonight. She should rise today. If she was able to change. I squashed the nugget of doubt and walked into the room. I placed my hand on her softly rounded cheek. It was cold. No sign of life, yet.

"No, Mark. But, she will raise today I am sure of it. Has there been any news from our leaks within the Coven?" We had infiltrated the Coven right before I killed Delaney.

"No, sir. But, the girl, she will rise, right?" Mark's voice was unsure. The pack was restless. They knew what was on the line and if they didn't agree, they needed to shut the fuck up about it.

"Yes, she will. And, Mark, spread the word - if anyone else calls me, they better be dying. Or they soon will be." I hung up the phone. I did not answer to my pack; they answered to me. What would they do? Kill me? I was the maker of ninety percent of them. It was physically impossible for a wolf to kill its maker.

I walked over to Delaney and stared at her dead form on the bed. Even in death, she was beautiful. Her curves were soft and begged for me to touch them. Her skin was a beautiful shade of cream with a slight blush to it. I yearned to see her full of life again. I fully expected her to hate me above all people, but she would get over it. I needed to use her to bring down the Coven.

There was a large brown leather chair next to the bed and I sank into it. I had spent much of the recent days and nights in this chair with hopes that Delaney would indeed rise. If it did not happen today, the chances of her rising were greatly diminished. I crossed my arms over my chest and began to plot. I had to be sure there were no loose ends to tie up.

Reid was the biggest loose end. I could just kill him and, man, I wanted to. He was more dominant than I, and in a fair fight I would be willing to bet he could take me. It was a good thing I made a practice of not fighting fair. When Delaney woke, she would be assured Reid was still alive. There was that old adage, "You can lead a horse to water, but you can't make him drink." Well, I had to make Delaney do as I wished. Holding Reid over her head was going to be the only way I could do that. I had to keep that smug bastard alive.

I smiled at the thought of Reid. He would have never guessed his only friend in the world would be the one killing people. He was as naive as Delaney, thinking she knew the whole prophecy. There was so much she didn't know. That whiny bitch of a great aunt made this so easy. She tried to keep Delaney out of danger so much, she neglected telling her anything. It was so easy to let them just simmer in their own stupidity.

I leaned up and rested my hands on the bed. I watched her chest for a telltale rise and fall, but there was nothing.

I often fantasized about her. It pissed me off to know she chose Reid. I would kill him eventually, but right now he would be my little pawn.

I pulled out my cell phone and glanced at the screen. It read 8:23 P.M. The last of the sun's yellow rays had just set. The night's sky was just coming into view. I got up and leaned over her.

Her lips were full, but not so much that they looked fake. Her dark-brown lashes fanned on her cheeks, begging to be kissed. I let my eyes do something I had been fighting since she was put on this bed in my house. I let them wander down her body. She was still dressed in the bloodstained white dress she had worn when we went out. The sight of that dress reminded me of what her blood tasted like and I groaned out loud. I loved the thrill of the chase, but for me the real thrill came with the taste of the kill. The feel of a pulse ending under my jaws. That rush of warm blood filling my mouth. And Delaney's blood had been different from any other blood I had before. She had tasted like power. A power I wanted to control. A power I couldn't help but be envious of.

I could just reach out and touch her, cup her. It took all my willpower not to grab at her. I reached a finger and ran it along the smooth skin on the tops of her breasts. I snatched my finger from her skin as if it burned me. It hadn't, but getting a hard-on from a dead girl wasn't the plan.

"Delaney, I have big plans for you. It's time to wake up."

Nothing happened. I didn't expect it to, really. I leaned over her face, only a few inches from our noses touching. This was absurd; I was acting like a child. I took one more glance at her luscious chest and then back at her eyes.

Looking back at me were glowing silver eyes.

"Hello, Delaney."

ABOUT EMILY CYR

EMILY CYR is a stay-at-home mom turned writer. She holds a degree in middle grades education with certification in English and social science. She has always had a love of all things paranormal and fantasy, but it wasn't until Emily's husband said the words, "Why not?" that she considered putting her thoughts and ideas into the book, The Lightning Prophecy. This trilogy was just the start for Emily. It seemed to open a creative door that had been locked.

Emily has always been an avid reader. Through reading came her love of writing. The more she read, the more she knew she wanted to create her own world. Many of her first works were fan fiction.

Emily and her family currently reside in Jacksonville, Florida. She has an incredibly supportive husband. They have two sons, ages 2 and 3. Somehow, even with the demands of being a parent to two little boys, she finds time to escape to her fantasies and write them down.

Though this is Emily's first published book, it will not be her last. She is currently working on book two in the Lightning Witch Trilogy and book one in the Vampire Favors series, titled Push and Pull.

All information regarding book signings and release dates can be found on her Facebook page: **www.facebook. com/EmilyCyrAuthor**

Made in the USA
Lexington, KY
23 August 2017